Ridin' Lonesome

B. N. Rundell

Ridin' Lonesome

B. N. Rundell

Wolfpack Publishing
P.O. Box 620427
Las Vegas, NV 89162

Print Edition ISBN: 978-1-64119-158-6

Dedication

Although the author seems to get all the credit, there is so much more that goes into a book than most realize. For me, I wouldn't be able to accomplish near enough without the encouragement and inspiration from my beloved wife, who is always by my side, patiently listening as I bounce ideas and characters around and always willing to provide an encouraging word or correction when needed. Although my children are not avid readers, they still encourage their old man and share my work with others. And the folks at Wolfpack publishing, Mike Bray and Rachel Del Grosso specifically, and the other "behind the scenes" workers, thank you. This story is taken from actual events of my Grandfather and Grandmother, but the details have been "modified" to make the account a little more interesting. Once again, thanks to all that have made this possible, and I dedicate this work to all of you.

Chapter One

Remembering

THE SHUFFLING GAIT of the steel dust gelding harmonized with the slumped shoulders of its rider. The mid-morning sky was littered with stretched out clouds with grey underbellies that threatened an early spring shower. Every step of the horse brought dust clouds that looked like miniature crowns for the slow moving hooves. A thin layer of dust blended the colors of the slouched felt hat and leather vest and shotgun chaps worn by the stoop shouldered young man aboard the well-used saddle. The scene could have been painted by an artist with nothing but greys and browns on his palette.

Even the surrounding terrain was devoid of any color but the dust covered grey of the sage and the cactus. Sadness painted the face that was hidden under the dusty hat and the Lindsey Woolsey shirt did little to hide or amplify the frame that bore it. The fringed chaps rested on the small rowels of his spurs as the toes of his scuffed boots pushed against the wooden stirrups. There was nothing impressive about the man as to his size or build or even the features of his face. He could stand unnoticed in a crowd and unremembered afterwards. His direction was uncertain and his future unplanned. But now on this little used trail across the rolling hills of the sagebrush covered plains, he let his mind travel the trails of his past.

His family, the Harpolds, had moved from Arkansas to Missouri in the early 1840's. Shortly after settling in to their small farm house, his dad felt the call to the ministry and began studying with the pastor of the little country church near their home. He occasionally filled the pulpit when the pastor was busy at other churches on his circuit and was always well-received with his practical sermons and personal applications.

The small community of Hillsboro was home to the Harpolds for almost a decade when his father believed God was calling him to go out West to provide spiritual guidance to the many settlers building towns in the frontier. With that call, the family packed up and headed to St. Louis, caught up with a wagon train and started their trek to the West. But an attack by some Pawnee as the wagon train crossed the plains following the Platte River, took a toll of several of the travelers, his father included.

He and his mother continued with the train, but before they reached Ft. Laramie, his mother joined his father. He was convinced she died of a broken heart since his father and mother had been together since they were children and had been married almost twenty-five years when he was killed. At Ft. Laramie, John William Harpold, known as J.W., sold the wagon and gear and most of his father's books. J.W. was well mounted on a steel dust gelding with long legs and good lungs that made him the envy of many. With a Colt Navy revolver riding in his home-made holster, a Sharps .52 caliber rifle nestled in a scabbard under the fender of his saddle, a bedroll with a change of clothes behind the cantle and some supplies and extra gear in his saddle bags, and a big bay pack horse with a few books, his bible and other essentials, he decided to head out on his own. Where exactly, he didn't know, but he knew he had to be alone for a while and he pointed his horse South West and started riding lonesome.

Just shy of seventeen, his "growing up" years had been spent in the woods of Arkansas and Missouri and did most of the hunting to provide meat for the family. With a neighbor that was a crusty old mountain man, he learned much about taking care of himself in forbidding circumstances and environments. But the terrain and people of the wilderness held little similarity to those of the Mid-West. Where the Ozarks were thickly forested with hard wood leafy trees, the plains were sparsely covered with scrub pinion, juniper, cedar and plenty of cacti. And of course, his knowledge of the many Indian tribes of the area was, at best, very limited.

He resolved to try to make his way to the mountains as quickly as possible and was following the guidance of an experienced but aging mountaineer he met at Ft. Laramie. He said his name was Jim Bridger as he told him, "Now you jist head on South West, keep them thar mountains off yore right shoulder. You kin foller the Laramie River out yonder, but it bends a bit North, course if'n ya take the first fork ya come to, that'll be the Chugwater River, ya kin foller it to the headwaters then bear West till ya hit the Laramie agin. And then ya kin foller the Laramie to its headwaters an' the first mountains ya come to will be them little ol' Medicine Bow Mountains, jus' stay to the South of 'em, and the next ones you'll see'l be the Gore Range.

Or ya could take a trail West 'bout thar an' that'll take ya over a couple a passes an' you'll git to the Gore range a little quicker. Now them's a bit bigger but they still run North n' South and then become the Sawatch Range. When they make a sharp turn to the East, that's when they become the Sangre De Cristo's. Now, that's 'bout where you'll run into the Arkansas River. If'n ya want, you can foller it downstream to Bent's Fort where ol' Billy'll be glad to re-supply ya, if'n ya need to. Course you can slip o'er them mountains and find the Rio Grande and foller it all the way to Sante Fe."

J.W. had memorized everything Bridger told him and was now using that as a mental map as to his direction. He really

3

didn't have any place else to go and they said the farther South you go, the warmer it'll be, so he was all for some warm weather. Suddenly his horse stopped, lifted his head and with ears forward warned his rider to pay attention. In the distance, about three hundred yards, several head of antelope were lazily grazing on scattered patches of buffalo grass. Although it was spring, the green had not come on the grass, but the antelope were not too particular of the color. J.W. had learned a little about the antelope on the trip out with the wagon train when the scout had taken him on a couple of hunts.

He kneed his mount to a small shoulder of a nearby rise, dismounted and carefully made his way to the top of the knoll. Watching the antelope until they were facing away from him, he then stepped to the top of the rise, sat down with crossed legs, loosened his neckerchief and let it blow in the wind and waited. Sitting very still with his readied Sharps across his lap, he watched. With nothing moving but his neckerchief, the antelope eventually became curious and casually began to make their way closer to the newcomer. After almost a half an hour, J.W. thought the animals were close enough, and carefully timing his moves when they had their heads down eating, he slowly raised his rifle to take aim. A young buck was to the near side and broad side to him as he squeezed off his shot.

The resulting explosion startled all the animals and with one collective move they launched themselves in their escape and within moments disappeared over the far hillsides leaving their downed companion to the hunter. J.W. made short work of field dressing the antelope, leaving the gut pile, head and legs for the scavengers and placed the carcass across the rump of his horse, strapped it down and mounted up to continue his journey, knowing he'd have fresh meat for his supper.

Following Bridger's directions, he was on the East bank of the Chugwater river bearing south and enjoying the scenery. He marveled at the rimrock formations that crowned the mesas and plateaus that surrounded him. The rock formations made him think, *It looks like God just crowned those hills with a row of standing rocks, then wrapped a robe of green pinery around their shoulders.* It was a big land he was traveling through and every new vista brought amazement and a touch of wanderlust to his heart and mind. This country was so different from what he had known in Arkansas and Missouri, even the animals were unique to this country.

The old mountain man back East who was his mentor had told many tales about Elk bugling, Mule Deer and their funny bouncing gait, big horn sheep and their bold curled horns, massive Grizzly bear that stood ten feet tall, these flat-land antelope with their unusual markings and speed, and J.W. knew he was falling in love with the West.

But repeated thoughts of losing his parents on their trip West still brought anger boiling to the surface, he just couldn't understand why God would call his Pa to the ministry and to come out West, just to be killed by the Indians. *It just don't make no sense to me.* Turning his face heavenward he cried out, "Why God! Why couldn't you keep 'em alive so he could do what he thought you wanted him too?" The echo of his angered plea made him realize he had yelled out loud and he immediately looked around to see if there was anyone within hearing distance. *Oh great, stupid, why don't you announce your presence to every Indian in the woods?*

Bridger had warned him about the Arapaho and Cheyenne that lived in this country and that he needed to be extra careful about making it too easy for them to find him. "Always travel as quiet as you can, boy. Them Injuns'll watch ya and they can tell if yore a greenhorn or not and there's nuthin' they'd like better than to hang yore topknot from their lance. So always travel easy 'n quiet like."

5

Chapter Two

Ute

THE STARS IN THE Eastern sky had just tucked themselves in and the three quarter moon slowly descended below the treetops in the west when J.W. lazily cracked open one eye to watch the dancing gold on the pines before him. Thinking it was the reflection from the rising sun, he tried to sneak in a little more sleep and closed his eye to shut out the light. Something niggled in his mind and both eyes popped wide open, seeing the brightness of the light dancing on the trees, he realized it wasn't from the sunrise and could only be from the campfire, but the campfire had burnt down in the night and should be nothing more than a bed of glowing embers.

He rolled over quickly onto one elbow and looked at the flaring fire and a figure seated on the log opposite him. Jumping up and grabbing for his Colt, he stepped to the side of the fire to confront the invader to his camp. He stopped and stared at a grey haired man bent over and tending the fire with a long stick that turned to smile at J.W.

"Morning sleepyhead," said the old man from behind a wrinkled and weathered face. Grey braids fell to his shoulders and rested on a buckskin vest that stretched across a bare chest that bore several scars. "I made some coffee, but I am not too good at it," he shared as he pointed with the stick toward to coffee pot at the edge of the fire.

"What are you . . .who . . . what . . ." stuttered J.W. as he waved the Colt around.

"I am NightHawk of the Muache Ute. I am traveling back to my people for the Bear dance to welcome the new season."

Seeing no threat from the old man, J. W. started to relax a little and lowered his pistol to his side, "Well, what . . . how come you stopped at my camp?" he said somewhat exasperated.

"My horse stepped in the hole of a whistle pig, what you white men call a prairie dog, and broke its leg. I was walking," he motioned with his stick to the North West, "and saw the glow of your fire last night. When I arrived you were asleep. I thought about taking your horses, but I thought you might die out here all alone, so I waited."

"That was mighty thoughtful of you, I guess. How far do you have to go to your people?"

"By horseback, one more day. But if this old man must walk, maybe two days."

J.W. stood looking at the old man and thinking about what he should do and was reminded of his father's words, "*Any man that crosses your path is there because God either made it happen or allowed it to happen, so we must always be ready to tell them about our God. Sometimes that will mean we have to help them or spend time with them, but we should always be willing to do whatever God allows or leads us to do.*"

But as he remembered, he also thought, *But I'm not the one that was supposed to be called to the Indians as a missionary, that was Pa!*"

The change of expressions on the young man's face and the nervous movement of his feet were not missed by the old man who said, "You fight with yourself about something, but if you sit down and have some coffee, maybe something to eat, you will think better."

Surprised at the old man's perception, J.W. let out a sigh and stuffed the Colt behind his belt and bent to pick up his tin cup and poured some coffee. As he sat on the nearby rock, he looked at Nighthawk and asked, "Did you have some coffee?"

The Indian smiled and said, "There is only one cup."

J.W. jumped up, went to the packsaddle and returned with another cup for the old man. He smiled gratefully and stretched out to retrieve the coffee pot and poured himself a cup.

After gazing glassy-eyed at the fire, J.W. looked up at the old man and said, "I have two horses!" to the understanding smile and nod of the old man. "Course you knew that already, but what I mean is we can rearrange the packs an you kin ride the pack horse to where you're goin', but you can't have him!" declared the enthusiastic green horn. "That is, ifn' it'd be safe fer me to go to your camp?" questioned J.W.

The old man looked at J.W., slowly smiled knowingly and said, "It would be good for you to come to my people. There are things you can learn about the mountains and others."

"How d'ya know I don't already know all I need to know?" asked J.W., feeling insulted by the implied remarks.

The Indian slowly smiled and looked at the young man and said, "When I came, I saw you had too big a fire that anyone, even an enemy could see," and motioning toward the packs and other gear, "you are not ready to leave, if you have to, in a hurry. Your rifle is still in the pack and it took you a while to find your pistol. I could have killed you many times before you woke, and this tells me you are not accustomed to living in the wilderness where not everything and everyone is your friend."

J.W.'s shoulders slumped as he realized the man spoke the truth. He had been careless and there was a lot for him to learn, if he lived long enough. The old man continued, "My people are known for their warlike ways and have taken many lives of their enemies. If a hunting party of my people or the Cheyenne or Arapaho had found you, you would now be with your ancestors."

"So if I come with you, let you ride my pack horse, your people will not attack me? And maybe you'll teach me some ways of the mountains and your people?"

"Yes. And you will see how we welcome the season with the Bear Dance as well."

J.W.'s wilderness education began almost immediately as they traversed a heavily timbered slope following a narrow game trail. The old man pointed out the antler rubs from the elk and deer as they passed through a thicket of Aspen that was showing the green buds of spring. As the trail continued into the spruce and pine woods, Nighthawk pointed to the scars from a Grizzly, "That is a big bear and those claw marks tell every other bear how big he is," and pointing to the edge of the scars he said, "That is his hair," and as he picked a long hair, he showed it to J.W. and said, "See the white? He is a silver-tip and wise and old like me. A bear that size can kill your horse with one swipe of his big paw and can take your head in his jaws." Then he lifted his head and sniffed the air, "He is not here," proclaimed the old man.

"You mean you can smell 'em?" asked J.W. skeptically.

"Yes, if you learn, you can smell the bear and even the elk also."

Mid-afternoon found the duo approaching the edge of the wide mesa like clearing that held the camp of the Utes. The wickiups, round dome-shaped pole framed dwellings, dominated the camp but a few hide teepees were scattered throughout. The Ute were not as nomadic as the plains Indians and preferred the more permanent dwellings but could still easily and quickly move if warranted. At the sight of the approaching visitors and the recognition of Nighthawk, several people greeted them and made them welcome. Nighthawk was the medicine man or shaman of the people and his return was

9

a source of joy for the people. He and his companion were escorted to his wickiup and a young woman soon joined them to start a fire and begin the preparation of a meal. J.W. later learned the young woman was the daughter of Nighthawk and the mother of his grandchildren, but she lost her husband to some unexplained illness and was now without a man to provide for her and was dependent on the generosity of the people. J.W. was to learn the Ute were a very compassionate people and always took care of those that were in need in any way.

While Spotted Bird prepared the meal, J.W. busied himself unpacking his gear. Nighthawk watched as the young man stacked some books near the outside wall and then carefully placed the last book on top of the stack. He smiled as he watched the special care given by the young man. "I see you have the white man's Bible. Do you know that book well?"

Surprised the Indian would recognize the Bible and know anything about it, J.W. responded, "It was my father's, he believed God was calling him to come West and share the truths in that book with the Indians, but he was killed before he could do that."

"And will you do that for him," inquired Nighthawk.

"God was calling him, not me," replied J.W. with sadness in his voice.

"But do you know the truths in the book?"

"Well, yes I do. I've taught the truths to others when I was in my father's church, but I'm no missionary," declared J.W.

"When I found you, I was returning from a visit with my sister who is with the Yoowetum Utes in the West. There was a white man, you said missionary, called Selman, who was teaching the people the truths from the Bible and my sister said her people were learning about your God. I teach you about our people and the mountains. Will you teach us about your God?"

J.W. was speechless as he looked at the old man. Never did he think of the possibility of following in his father's

10

mission calling. He did not believe God had called him to teach the Indians and he did not believe he could. But the remembered words of his father continued to ring in his mind as he thought about this sharing of the truths. Looking at the sincere question written in the eyes of Nighthawk, J.W. considered the idea and finally answered the old man, "I suppose I could, for a while. But just a few days, then I've got to be movin' on. I'm on my way to Texas and that's a long way." As he spoke it, he had no idea where it came from because he hadn't settled it in his own mind as to where he was going, but now that it was out in the open, maybe that was where he meant to go. But not right away, now he had an obligation to fulfill to the people of Nighthawk.

Chapter Three

Teaching

AT THE INSTRUCTION of Nighthawk, Spotted Bird readied a pot of coffee for the visitor to her people. Awakened by the smell of the brewing coffee, J.W. took a few moments to orient himself to the dimly lit interior of the wickiup. Rolling over to see the woman at the fire, he received a smile of greeting as she motioned for him to partake of her first pot of coffee. He gladly emerged from his bedroll, slipped on his boots and after running a hand through his thick thatch of hair, he grabbed his cup and poured java to the brim. Speaking in her native tongue of Shoshonean and sign language, she made herself understood as she offered a wooden bowl of some sort of meal for his breakfast. Realizing the barrier of languages, he was relieved to see Nighthawk return and join him for the meal. When they finished their second cup of coffee, Nighthawk asked J.W. to join him for a walk and some more teaching.

As they walked through the nearby woods on a circuitous route, Nighthawk casually used every moment as a teaching opportunity. He would point out different plants and their use and focused especially on the Osha plant or Bear plant. "This is a very good plant for many uses. We make a tea from it, use its leaves for wounds and when we travel in the dry land we rub it on to keep rattlesnakes away." As he spoke, he lifted the leaves almost reverently and added, "Do not take it without giving thanks to the Creator." J.W. enjoyed the walk and the teaching and listened attentively to the elder to absorb all the knowledge that was being shared. He noticed their walk was again nearing the village as Nighthawk began to share his people's story of their beginnings. "The bear is important to our people in many ways, it was from the cave of the bear that first man emerged and our people began. Tell me the story of your God and the beginning of the white man," he asked.

"Well, in our Bible, God starts with '*In the beginning . . .*' and my father would take from the book of Job, '*In the beginning God stood upon nothing, because there was nowhere to stand, and reached out where there was nowhere to reach and caught something from nothing. Then he flung it toward the blackness and hung the stars to light the night, and then molding with his hands he formed the sun to light the day. Then God said, It is good.*' His Word, the Bible, tells us how he created man and woman and all the animals and everything. But He talks about man as all men, not just white men and red men or others, but man." As J.W. spoke, he didn't notice that Nighthawk continued to lead them on their trek and they were actually making another circuit around the entire camp. All the while J.W. spoke, Nighthawk listened intently and occasionally nodded his head or asked a question but it was evident he was very interested in all J.W. said. At the end of their second circuit, Nighthawk motioned for them to return to the wickiup and to sit outside to continue their discussion.

As they visited, sometimes teaching, sometimes learning, J.W. noticed the increasing activity of the village as more and more families arrived and erected their teepees and established their camp. A group of the men were busy building what J.W. thought was a large corral he assumed would be for the many horses of the visitors. All the while, he enjoyed the time with

Nighthawk and continued in his narrative of the many truths of the Bible. When he spoke of the sacrifices from the book of Leviticus, a troubled Nighthawk quizzed him about the need for the sacrifices and J.W. explained, "I believe God did that so the people would understand that sin, or doing wrong, has a cost to it, it's what happens in our life and the lives around us when we do things that hurt us and our friends and family." Nighthawk thought about that and countered with, "The Great Spirit of our people does not ask for sacrifice but we know that wrongdoing does bring much pain."

Nighthawk stood as if to signify the teaching time was over and walked away, leaving J.W. wondering about the man and his people. With nothing to occupy his time, he decided to busy himself with cleaning his rifle and pistol and organizing his packs. As he was seated outside and cleaning his rifle, he was approached by a young man of about ten or twelve who stood with arms crossed and looked at the white man curiously. As J.W. continued to clean the rifle, he motioned for the young man to be seated on the nearby log and watch. When J.W. reassembled his rifle, he lifted it to his shoulder and showed the young man how to hold it. When the young man started to lift it, he was surprised at the weight and looked in askance to J.W. as he chuckled. Nighthawk returned and explained to the young man about the rifle and received a broad smile of recognition in return. Looking to J.W., Nighthawk said, "Rabbit asked to shoot your rifle but I told him no because it would scare the people." J.W. rubbed the boy on the top of his head and the young man trotted off to tell his friends about the white man's rifle.

Seating himself at a woven willow back rest Nighthawk began to explain to J.W., "In the morning, we will begin the final preparations for the Bear dance. The people will gather for the story and then we will have the dance at the corral and after we will have a feast."

"I've seen a lot of people coming and joining the village, who are they?" inquired J.W.

"All are Ute, but from other bands," pointing at a newly erected teepee he added, "Those are Tabeguache, those over there are the Parianuche from far over the mountains, and there are others as well. The Bear dance is to honor the time when Mother Earth begins to renew and bears come out of their dens and all our people want to celebrate that, but it is a good time to see family and friends too," he said, smiling to imply one main purpose of the dance was to socialize. "It is a time when young people can make happy unions and find a mate."

The following morning the people began to assemble in the large central area of the village. Nighthawk had left early but told J.W. to watch and enjoy the festivities of the day. A raised platform had been constructed near the edge of the corral and Nighthawk appeared dressed in colorful beaded buckskin leggings, breechcloth, a fringed tunic and feathers and tufts of fur in his braids. He raised his hands and began, "Long, long ago two brothers were hunting in the mountains and could not find game. After walking a great distance, they were tired and sat down to rest. One brother jumped up when he saw a big bear standing before a tree and looked like he was dancing and talking to the tree and clawing at it. The other brother left to do more hunting but the first brother stayed and watched the bear. When he was alone, the bear looked at the man and began to teach him to do the same dance and also taught him the song that he was singing. Then our brother Bear told him to return to the people and teach them the dance and the songs of the bear. These songs teach us to show respect for the spirit of our brother the bear and the woods where he lives. Now, go forth and dance."

All the people scampered to the corral, formed two lines with the men in one and the women in the other and all began to chant the words of the song as the drummers beat the cadence and the flutists played the music. J.W. watched and Nighthawk joined his young friend and explained, "You see they all have plumes or feathers and when the dance is over they will leave those on the cedar tree there at the East to show they leave their troubles behind them and start their new season of life. Now, isn't that better than making a sacrifice like your God required?"

"Yes, it is, if that was all that was done. But you see, God did more. In the rest of the Bible, He tells how he sent his own son, to be the sacrifice to pay for our sins," shared J.W.

Nighthawk looked at the young man with a confused expression and asked, "You mean your God made his own son a sacrifice? He died?"

"That's right, but even though Jesus, God's Son died for our sins, it didn't end there. God raised Jesus from the dead and He lives on High now. He paid the price for our sin so we don't have to, but God says we must believe with all our heart in what Jesus did for us and that He purchased the gift of eternal life for us so all we have to do is accept that gift and we will live forever in Heaven with Him," explained J.W.

Nighthawk thought for a moment and asked, "So the sacrifice paid for our sin or bad things and bought a gift for us? A gift that lets us live forever in Heaven?"

"That's right. So there are no more sacrifices, just believing in Him with our whole heart," shared J.W. as he pointed toward Heaven.

Nighthawk slowly nodded his head, looked at J.W. to determine his sincerity and slowly walked away as he pondered his most recent lesson.

J.W. finished strapping down the gear on the pack horse, went to his horse and checked the gear to ensure all was properly secured, grabbed the saddle horn and wiggled the saddle to further check, slipped the Sharps into the scabbard and turned to Nighthawk to say his goodbyes. As Nighthawk looked at the young man he asked, "This gift you spoke of, the one that lets you live forever on the other side, how do I get it?"

"Just ask for it. You see, Nighthawk, God is always watching and listening and all we have to do is pray, something like this, *Dear God, forgive me of my sins and give me the gift of life forever with you, please come and live in my heart.* It's not the words you say, but what you feel in here," he said as he tapped the man on the chest. "Do you understand what I mean?"

Nighthawk nodded his head and let a smile stretch the corners of his mouth to blend with the many other wrinkles. Putting his hand on the shoulder of his young friend, he said, "I understand, and I will do that. But you must come back and teach us more and I will teach you too."

As J.W. stepped into the stirrup and lifted himself into his saddle, he looked back at the old man and said, "If the good Lord brings me back, we'll teach each other." Nodding his head, he waved good bye and kneed his horse to the trail heading South and once again J.W. found himself riding lonesome.

Chapter Four

Company

THE SPLASHING AND CHUCKLING white water of the swift moving Arkansas River beckoned to the dusty traveler. After well over a week of riding on dusty trails and meandering paths, J.W. felt the dirt and the smelled the stench of his long unwashed body. With the long day fading into dusk, he decided to make an early camp and make a few changes. The copse of cottonwood and willow by the riverbank invited his attention and he easily decided the small glen would be a satisfactory campsite. His camp preparation had become routine and his pack, bedroll, saddle, and gear were soon in their customary place as he looked longingly at the placid pool of backwater near the grassy bank. Stripping down to his drawers, he carried his clothing in a stack with a large bar of lye soap and walked into the pool of cold water. "Whooooeeee," he said to no one in particular, "That thar water is plum cold!" He quickly lathered up his britches, shirt and long johns, swirled them in the pool to rinse, wrung them out and tossed them on the bank. He squatted in the shallow water to soak a mite and dipped his shaggy head under. Coming up with a splutter and sucking a deep breath, he started scrubbing with the bar of soap and began humming to himself. A good day of traveling was topped off with a much needed soaking and scrubbing. With another dip to rinse his head, he stood and started for the bank.

"Well, hello there!" rang the greeting through the small glade and brought J.W. to a sudden stop as he froze where he stood waist deep in the water. Goose bumps were fighting for attention across his chest and down his arms and a bone jarring shudder told of his discomfort. He searched for the source of the greeting and was surprised to see what appeared to be a young woman, but she was attired in baggy britches and a sagging shirt under a floppy hat that obscured everything but the long blonde hair that tumbled to her shoulders.

"You might not wanna come outta there 'till ya get yore britches on," she giggled.

He looked down at his bare chest, back up at her and crossed his arms across his nakedness and said, "I would, but they're layin' there on the bank," motioning to a pile of his clean change of clothes. She looked where he motioned, smiled and returned with, "O.K., I'll turn around." When she showed him her back, he quickly waded to the shore, grabbed his clothes and started dressing. As he was doing up his Lindsey Woolsey shirt, he asked, "Where'd you come from? I didn't think there was anybody around for days."

Speaking over her shoulder she said, "Ah, we got us a farm started just over yonder a spell. Just finished the cabin this summer and ain't got much in the way of crops yet, but Pa's got big ideas."

"A farm? Out here? There ain't nothin' can grow here but sagebrush, buffalo grass, cactus and rattlesnakes. Where'd ya come from, anyway?" he asked as he walked to her side.

"I tol' ya! From our farm over yonder."

"No, I mean before that. You know, where was yore home 'fore ya came out here?"

"Oh, Ohio. We had us a farm there but couldn't raise nuthin' but rocks, so Pa joined up with a wagon train, but when we got to Independence, we took South on the Sante Fe trail while them others, Mormons they was, went North to the Emigrant trail."

"Well, I'm fixin' to have me some supper, you can join me if ya' like."

With a nod of her head, she followed J.W. to the well-used fire ring. This site had been used by travelers before, probably Indians as well as others, but J.W. was comfortable with the site and the far-ranging visibility across the flats. He tossed his Bowie knife at the feet of the girl and instructed, "Cut a couple a' willows sticks fer skewering steaks oer' the fire." She looked at him, bent and picked up the knife and went to the willows to secure their skewers. J.W. started the campfire and worked to prepare some cornpone, and tossed some yampa roots in the frying pan and set it near the fire. The girl returned with two trimmed willow skewers and J.W. put the last two slices of the back strap from the deer on to suspend them over the fire.

"Say, what is your name anyway?" asked J.W. as he sat on the large rock near the fire where he could tend the cooking.

"Kacee, name's Kacee, Kacee Melissa Thacker. My Pa named me after a town back home. Said my name was gonna be Kacee ifn' I was a boy or a girl."

"Did he ever decide?" asked J.W. with a mischievous smile.

"Decide what?"

"Whether you was a boy or a girl."

She quickly snatched up a stick and threw it at him but he knocked it away with his arm and chuckled at her response.

"That weren't nice, not nice at'all," she pouted.

"Ah, I'se just joshin' ya. I knowed all along you was a girl, your long hair gave it away! How old are you anyway?"

"I'm goin' on fourteen," she stated emphatically with arms crossed in front of her chest.

"Twelve's more like it."

"Hummmph, a lot you know, you ain't very old your own self!" she stated.

J.W. took a big swig of coffee to top off his meal and looked at his company and asked, "Say, how far's that Bent's fort? I thought I'd be runnin' into it pretty soon."

"Keep follerin' the river and you'll run into it all right. Ain't but a short ways downriver, but why'd ya wanna go there? Ain't nuthin' there no more."

"Whatdya mean, ain't nuthin' there? I was told I could re-supply there with ol' Wm. Bent his own self," asked J.W., confused.

"Ahh, it sat empty fer a while, so they say, then Bent burnt it and moved his stuff down ta' Big Timbers. He's got a tradin' post down there. Ain't too much further, maybe half a day."

"Well, I'll be durned, things sure do change in a hurry nowadays, don't they?"

Kacee jumped up and said, "Well, I gotta be gittin' on home now. Pa'll have a conniption fit if I ain't there by dark. You keep your top knot on now, ya' hear?" With a quick wave she trotted off and was out of sight before J.W. could even say good bye. He shook his head and cleaned up the plates and pans and readied himself for his usual move. After the lessons learned from Nighthawk, he had made it a practice to have his supper with a small fire, then move his camp at least a mile away before turning in for the night.

Just shy of mid-day, J.W. tethered his horse at the hitch rail in front of the log cabin with the trading post sign over the door. He looked at the cluster of teepees to the side of the cabin and watched the different activities of the Indian families. Kids were playing some game with sticks and a ball of some kind of fur, women were tending pots suspended over cook fires, and men were lounged in front of the teepees reclining on the woven willow back rests. A few of the men returned his gaze as he started to enter the log cabin. The dimly lit interior revealed a long plank across a couple of barrels that served as a counter and countless shelves along the walls that seemed to be overflowing with trade goods. Two men rested on their elbows as they swirled their drinks in the small glasses but didn't pay any attention to the visitor. J.W. approached the counter and was greeted by a potbellied man with buckskin breeches held up by shoulder straps that stretched over the paunch. A plaid drop shoulder shirt was rolled up at the sleeves and open at the chest. Removing a clay pipe from between pudgy lips, a squeaky voice asked, "What kin I do ye fer, stranger?"

J.W. rattled off his list of needed supplies, looked at the shelves for any after thoughts and waited while the trader piled his stuff on the counter. The two men were now watching the transaction with a bit of curiosity. J.W. asked the clerk if he was interested in any hides and the clerk responded with, "Whatcha got?"

"Well, I've got three antelope, four deer and one buffalo hide. They're out yonder on my pack horse, I salted 'em and rolled 'em up."

After reaching an agreement concerning the hides and supplies, J.W. settled up with the clerk and turned to leave when he was confronted by one of the two observers. "Say there friend, where you plannin' on goin' from here?"

"And who'd be askin' and why'd ya wanna know?"

"Oh, no offense, but me an' my partner here were headin' back to Texas and we're a little short on supplies, thought maybe we'd take on another partner so it'd be safer goin' through the territory."

"Territory?" asked J.W.

"Yeah, Indian territory. Since they moved all them Injuns from back East, the territory is where they been puttin' 'em all and it's got ta' where it ain't too safe crossin' there. Course we'd just be cuttin' cross a corner of it, but still . . . "

"So, why should I join up with you fellas? I've got plenty of supplies and I can go just 'bout anywhere I want to. But I was thinkin' 'bout Texas," he mused.

"Yeah, see there. Have you ever been to Texas?" asked the taller stranger.

"Nope, but I ain't got no place else to go. Say, didn't you say you were going back? Is that your home?"

"Closest thing we got to a home. We took a herd up to a place near Denver City and we're headin' back to the ranch where we work, the spear V, it's a purty good spread just South of Dallas a ways."

"Well, maybe we can join up, I was thinkin' 'bout visitin' some family down there, just South of a place called Waxa . . . waxa sumthin.. uh, Waxahachie. Ain't that kinda near to where you come from?" asked J.W.

"Sure is! Why it ain't but mebbe a couple days from our place. By the way, I'm Dusty and this here's Hank."

"And I'm J.W."

With a nod to the clerk, the three men left the trading post and mounted up to start their journey through Indian territory together. It is at such times that men oft make decisions that will change the course of their lives when they join with others to take a different trail. When brief acquaintance and quick judgment is in error, it is at such times that lives are surrendered. But when those choices are made with confidence and trust, those same lives are often enriched with friendships and adventure. Such was the time of J.W. and his new found companions, Dusty and Hank, men that would stand together or fail together, but their lives were now linked. Yet J.W. simply considered at least he was not riding lonesome.

Chapter Five

Territory

THE THREE MEN sat their saddles with their hands on the pommels and horns and stared at the slow moving muddy river that hindered their progress. "That's the Canadian! I told you back yonder when we crossed the Cimarron and the North Canadian that they weren't nuthin'! Now this here's a river an' the only thing bigger is the Red. Now that's a river! We grow 'em big here in Tejas, just like ever'thin' else, it's big all right," announced Dusty as he nodded his head and cackled like a hen that just laid an egg.

J.W. looked at the grinning Dusty and answered, "That ain't no river, that's just a crick compared to the Mississippi! Why even the Missouri, or the Big Mo as they call it, is bigger'n that piece of rollin' mud."

"Yore joshin' me ain'tcha? Them rivers ain't that big are they?" then turning to his partner, Hank, he said, "Tell him Hank, this hyar's a big 'un and so's the Red!"

"They're big all right Dusty, but from what I hear, those other'ns are bigger. But it don't make no never mind nohow. Come on, let's get 'crost for it's too dark." With that

24

declaration, Hank led the way for the trio and the pack horse to make their way across the river. The men sat easy and let the horses have their heads. The current was strong but not so fast as to cause concern and with the usual bobbing ride they made it safely to the South shore of the Canadian river. This was their fourth day since their joining and the companions found their common company tolerable, even enjoyable. The two Texans shared their stories of working on a cattle ranch and J.W. shared his tales of traveling and learning from the Ute Indians. Men often shared their hard earned knowledge with one another as their primary source of learning. Many of that time were unschooled and gained only a wilderness education by learning from others. J.W. was especially interested in the accounts of working with cattle for his father had often expressed his thoughts that the raising of cattle could become the best way for a man to make his fortune. He would say, " *J.W., I believe we'll see a civil war in our time what with the conflict over the keeping of slaves and other conflicting beliefs. And a growing nation will need food and meat and the farmers and ranchers will need to provide for the expanding hordes of people.* "

He remembered his father talking about an uncle that had gone to the Mexican lands that were called Tejas and founded a ranch. J.W. knew little about his uncle because that uncle was not a favored relative of the Harpold family, but J.W. never knew the reason. Since he joined his traveling partners, he had allowed himself to ponder the possibility of locating his uncle and maybe working with him on his ranch. But that was just a thought and nothing concrete to build a life upon.

After crossing the Canadian River, their route would take them South East until they hit the Red River. After crossing the Red, they would follow the South bank for four or five days, then swing South to hit the Brazos and follow it to their home country. Their destination would be about two or three days South East of Ft. Worth, the northernmost post of the seven forts established to protect the settlers. They would be traveling through what was widely considered to be Indian territory between the established Indian territory in what would later become Oklahoma and the forts built after the Mexican American war. Inhabited by the Comanche, Kiowa and Apache, the many raids into the settled countryside had taken their toll among the settlers. Hank and Dusty shared a few tales of the raids that happened before they took the herd North and now cautioned J.W. to ride watchful, ". . .cuz ya' cain't never tell about these Injuns. One day they'll be peaceable and friendly, and the next they're ready to cut yore throat and lift yo' hair! And them Comanch' is the worst!"

The first day after crossing the Red River the trio was looking for a bit of shade for their noon stop and to give the horses a bit of rest. Dusty stood in his stirrups and pointed to a small copse of Pecan and Hackberry with some low growing brush that appeared to be willows. "Up yonder looks likely, whatcha think?" he asked his companions. As he turned to get a response from them he hollered, "Holy Mackerel, Injuns!" and grabbed his hat and whipped his mount on the rear to head to the trees for cover. J.W. and Hank didn't waste time as the screams, yips and battle cries from the pursuers confirmed Dusty's alarm. With the three men hunkered over their pommels, their hats in hand as quirts to urge the horses to a faster flight, their legs and stirrups were flapping in the breeze as if they were wings, their elbows bouncing to ready for flight and each one sounding off with his own rebel yell before there was such a thing, they were a sight to behold.

J.W. snatched a look to see how close death followed and as his bushy locks caught the wind and tried to obscure his view, he recognized something that brought a Nighthawk lesson to mind. These were youngsters on a coup raid. They weren't brandishing weapons but were leaning down along the necks of their mounts and stretching out the long decorated and feathered coup sticks. J.W. jerked the reins on his mount and hollered at Hank, "Wait! They're just kids wantin' to count coup! Follow me!" He reined his horse around and charged headlong straight toward the advancing Comanche and within moments he could make out the startled looks on their faces as they sat up and reined their horses to a sliding stop. Before they could turn their mounts to retreat, J.W. and Hank had reached the young would-be warriors and snatched the coup sticks from them and bumped their horses against the surprised warrior's mounts. Then J.W. raised the long stick that reminded him of a shepherd's staff, over his head and brought it down on the shoulder of the young Comanche and Hank mimicked his action. The two partners laughed and threw the coup sticks to the ground and spun their mounts around and loped away to join Dusty that sat less than one hundred yards away with his mouth agape at the action of his friends. With a few glances over their shoulders to be certain there was no pursuit, the two men laughed all the way back to the waiting Dusty. "You fellers are plum loco. That had to be the dumbest stunt I ever seen anybody pull, why they coulda been ready to run you through and take yore hair! Ya'll are crazy, I tell you, crazy!"

Most of a week later they camped by the Brazos River where Dusty and Hank, now feeling the pull of their home stompin' grounds, continued to regale J.W. with tales of their adventures on the ranch. "I tell you what, J.W., them Mex Vaqueros is sumpin', they can do things with their riatas that just don' seem possible. Now, me and Hank are purty good hands with one, but them Vaqueros can just 'bout make it stand up an' dance. Why one time they was this rank ol' steer that didn't wanna come out o' the brush, an' ever onct in a while he'd lift his head up oer' the mesquite and kinda dare ya to come after him. Wal, that thar Vaquero just limbered out his riata, took one swing around his head and stretched that thing out seemed like it went most of a hunert feet and laid over that ol' steer's head and that Mex just dallied up and pulled him outta that brush just like they was goin' ta meetin' on a Sunday morning'! Yessir, if I'm lyin' I'm dyin' that's the way it was!" All the while he jabbered he coiled his riata, threw a loop, brought it back and coiled it again, unconscious of what he was doing, but giving his hands something to do while he talked.

After listening to the many tales of cowboying from the two homesick ranch hands, J.W finally asked, "Could you fellas teach me how to handle a rope like that? I mean, just in case I get hired on a ranch sometime?"

Hank chuckled at the question and responded, "We can show ya' a few things, but the only way you'll ever git ta' where you can use one of these things is with practice an' experience. We been doin' it nigh onto ten years our own selves and we ain't much. We both started when we was knee high to a grasshopper, but we'll gitcha started. I got a spare riata you can use, at least till we git to the bunkhouse."

Almost three weeks had been spent in the saddle by the three men that now considered themselves to be friends. With every day spent so close together, few secrets were held and most dreams were shared. Traveling, camping, hunting, and outrunning Indians provided the common ground for young men to forge fast friendships. J.W. had enjoyed seeing the new country with wide meadows painted with bluebells and a myriad of other flowers that raised their heads to the warmth of spring. These colors and vistas were a new experience for one whose youth had been spent in the close confines of hardwood forests and denser populations. But this country quickly grew on a man and J.W. found himself feeling at home in a place never visited before. Hank stopped the entourage as he raised his hand and then pointed to the distant buildings and corrals. "There it is! The Spear V! Boy howdy, it shore is good to be back. Wonder what ol' cooky's got on the fire fer supper?"

J.W. fidgeted uneasily in his saddle and Dusty noticing his discomfort said, "Well, J.W., I don't rightly know if the boss'll be able to take on 'nother hand, but we'll shore put in a good word fer ya. Ifn' he can't, he'll probly know of any places aroun' that could use another hand. But, you can at least stay here a day or two and git some more meat on yore bones, anyway."

"Yeah, I know, and I appreciate that. If he can't, that's all right, I'll make out."

When the men rode into the yard between the bunkhouse and the main house, they were welcomed by a couple hands at the corral and an older man that waved from the porch of the main house. Greetings were exchanged, and the trio made their way to the bunkhouse. They were followed by a weather beaten middle aged man with a sweat brimmed felt hat, a leather vest over a plaid wool shirt and gambler striped britches tucked into tall Mexican boots. He removed the cigarillo that was dangling from his lip and asked Hank and Dusty about their trip and why it took them so long to return. After giving explanations and excuses, Hank introduced J.W. and asked about the Spear V taking on a new hand. As Tom, the foreman, looked J.W. up and down, he said, "Fellas, I wish we could. We could use another hand ever now an' then, but the boss said we ain't takin' on any till roundup. But I did hear the McPherson's were lookin' to add a couple hands. Ya might try over there friend," suggested Tom, then continued, "Course ya oughta just have some vittles and stay the night cuz it'll take bout half a day ta' git thar."

With supper over, the men were sitting on the edge of the porch watching the sunset that covered the entire Western sky and shared tidbits of memories and stories. As dark settled over the flats, they retired to their bunks before the next day started sooner than the sun would rise. Come morning, with breakfast done, J.W. asked Tom if he ever heard of a place owned by someone name of Harpold. "Cain't say as I have, now I been here goin' on eight years so mighta been fore my time." Disappointed, J.W. said his goodbyes and with promises to meet again made, he waved over his shoulder as he followed the directions of Tom toward the McPherson spread and once again, he was riding lonesome.

29

Chapter Six

Mcpherson

TOPPING A SMALL juniper covered rise, J.W. stopped to take in the view of the wide valley below. It was a beautiful sight that greeted the visitor to the flats of central Texas, Bluebonnets provided a carpet of brilliant blue with a whisper of green and highlights of yellow and red. Adding to the color, a smattering of red and white cattle grazed lazily in the morning sun. These were the beginning of the mix breeds, the heavier and beefier English breeds crossed with the rangy hearty Mexican breed that sported bigger horns. When this mix-breed developed they would become the sizable and durable long horns that would make Texas famous. As far as J.W. could see to the East and South the scene continued unchanging. Deciding to take a noon break, J.W. dismounted and tethered his horse to the nearest Juniper. The long lead rope gave the horse ample area for graze and he wasted no time partaking of the greenery at his feet. J.W. found a perch to continue his survey of the countryside, the hard rock seemed to be carved out just for his comfort and he bent a knee to give an armrest, pushed his hat back on his head and took in the panorama like a refreshing drink to a starving desert traveler.

He sat for a while chewing on some dried deer meat and taking in everything from the cactus at his feet to the cloudless blue sky beyond the horizon. In the distance before him he noticed two men on horseback moving away and disappearing over a slight rise in the rolling terrain. Assuming they were ranch hands for the McPherson spread, he decided to follow. Standing and stretching, he strolled to his mount, unloosed the tethered lead rope, mounted up and reined his long legged steel dust gelding through the scattered rocks and juniper to the valley floor and pursued the two riders. Cresting the small knoll that obscured the trail before him, he stopped and gazed at the buildings that lay below. A large barn with hay hanging from the mow dominated while a long low structure, probably the bunkhouse, appeared as a little brother to the bigger barn. Set back a ways was a large two story adobe Spanish style house with a tile roofed veranda that reminded J.W. of the twirling skirt on a dancing woman. The reddish-brown building stood out this wild and beautiful country but somehow seemed to be a part of it all, with the dusky colors of the adobe matching that of the surrounding countryside. *Well, I'll be a monkey's uncle, I shore never expected to see a fine house like that out chere. Only place I ever saw a house that big was back in St. Louie,* thought J.W. Several corrals stretched out from the barn near the bunkhouse and were bordered by two smaller sheds, probably for storage or tack and just beyond stood what must be the cook shack. Behind the bunkhouse stood a solitary privy that matched the one behind the main house. The nearer corral held a good selection of horses and the larger corral stood empty. The entire setting was surrounded by a wall of a combination of adobe and poles and sported an entry gate with two tall posts and a cross bar that held what appeared to be a brand hanging from the center. For those that could read the brand it was the Lazy I M, the initials of the owner, Ian McPherson.

J.W. spurred his horse toward the gate and as he passed through he drew the stares of the two men he followed who were unsaddling their mounts outside the near corral. Another man was forking some hay over the fence to the horses. Sitting on a large rocking chair on the veranda was a sizable red-bearded man that surveyed the grounds like a foreign potentate observing his exclusive domain. Standing beside him with a hand resting on his shoulder was a long haired beauty of a girl of about sixteen or seventeen, and by the standards of the times she was a woman threatening to become an old maid. J.W. reined his horse to the corral and leaning on the pommel, asked the pitchfork holding hand, "Who's the ramrod?"

Looking up at the stranger, the man put his pitchfork tines to the ground and leaning on the handle responded, "And just who's askin'?"

"I'm J.W. an' Tom over at the Spear V sent me over, said you were looking to take on a few new hands. This is the McPherson place, ain't it?"

"Yup, it's the McPherson place, an' the ramrod is ol' Hoppy, but he's out with some o' the boys in the North pasture. But that's ol' man McPherson up on the porch, ya' might try talkin' to him," he instructed as he motioned with his chin toward the main house. Looking over his shoulder to the house, J.W. reined his horse around and walked it to the house. As he neared he spoke, "Mr. McPherson, Tom oe'r at the Spear V said you folks might be takin' on some new . . ." he was distracted by the spreading smile on the face of the girl at the big man's shoulder but quickly recovered and continued, ". . .uh, takin' on some new hands. Is that right?"

The patriarch stood and looked down at the man sitting his horse by the hitch rail and said, "Maybe laddie, but do ye have any experience workin' wit' cattle?"

"To be honest, no sir, but I spent the last three weeks with a couple of the boys from the Spear V makin' our way down from the mountains and they taught me a few things 'bout ropin' and such. What I don't know I could learn, I'm a pretty quick study."

Ian McPherson considered himself to be a good judge of character and he looked over the man before him. He liked what he saw in the man with an honest face and sincere eyes. J.W. had filled out some since he first took the trail from Ft. Laramie and now stood a good six feet with broad shoulders and strong hands that extended past the sleeves of the too small shirt. His shotgun chaps showed wear and the mount he rode was a well-muscled long legged horse that looked like he could go all day and still have some bottom left. The tall red-bearded broad chested man stuck his thumbs behind his belt and said, "What be ye name boy?"

"John Harpold sir, but most folks just call me J.W."

"Harpold? Did ye have any family here 'bouts?"

"Well, my Pa said he had a brother that had a ranch somewhere in this part of the country, but I never knew him or where he was," replied J.W.

"Humm, I remember a Harpold that had a place just South of here, but he's gone now and that place has gone back to grass," he looked as if he was remembering a long past time. Then looking up at J.W. he said, "All right sonny, I be givin' ye a chance ta' prove yerself. But ye be the bottom of the pile and all the hard jobs'll fall to ye. So, ye better make the best of 'em or it's soon ye be gone. Over yonder is the bunkhouse, go 'head on and putcha gear away. The boys'll tell ye when to make it to supper. Hoppy'll tell ye what ye be doin'" he stated as he dismissed his new hire by turning his back to him and stepping to the front door. The girl lingered a moment and with a timid smile at J.W., she bowed her head and followed her father into the house.

J.W. reined his horse around and went to the corral leading the pack horse. He stepped down and the man with the pitch fork approached and asked, "So, did he hire you on?"

"Yes he did, so looks like I'll be stayin' on a spell," answered J.W.

"Good, good. Now that means I ain't the low man on the totem pole and you get all the dirty jobs. Wheww . . . that's a relief, I've had it with muckin' stalls an' such. By the way, I'm Sidney, but most of 'em just call me Skinny cuz I ain't got much meat on my bones. You said you're called J.W.?" asked the tall slender man. J.W. looked him over and understood why they called him skinny. When he turned away, J.W. saw there was little difference between him and the pitchfork he carried. Skinny called over his shoulder, "I'll meetcha in the bunkhouse an' fill ya in on things."

When he entered the bunkhouse, Skinny was sitting on the bunk nearest the door and motioning to the bunk said, "This hyar's yore bunk. The new guy allus gits this'n cuz it catches the cold from the door and you're the one what's gotta get the firewood and start the fire in the mornin'. Course with summer gittin' hyar, that won't be much, but when the ramrod comes thru the door with some dirty job ta do, yore the first one what gits it!" he chuckled as he looked at the newcomer.

J.W. smiled as he dropped his gear beside the bunk and stretched, arching his back and looked over the interior. There were about a dozen bunks evenly spaced along the outside walls, most with gear stacked beside them. He asked Skinny, "Are there that many hands? Looks like a dozen bunks."

"Nah, that's when the ol' man adds some hands for roundup time. Now there's just you'n me, two others and the three sons o' ol man McPherson."

"You mean he makes his own sons sleep out here?" asked J.W. incredulously as he thought about the massive home where he saw the girl.

"Yeah, there's three of 'em an' the ol' man thinks they learn more by bein' outchere wit' the rest of us. They ain't so bad, well cep'n fer Patrick, he thinks he's top dog, but the other two, Sean and Shamus, they're all right. Say, soon's they all git back, Cook'll have supper ready an' we can git some chow. Should be purty soon, course Hoppy makes us work from can see to can't see, but it's comin' on dark soon," said Skinny as he stood in the open doorway looking at the setting sun.

Chapter Seven

Learning

THE EDUCATION OF THE new man began with a kick at the foot of his bunk to roust him out and to his job of starting the fire in the potbellied stove. The cool of the morning was not met with any enjoyment on the part of the lanky J.W. as he rolled out, slipped on his britches pulling the suspenders over his shoulders and driving his feet into his boots. With a quick rub of his whiskered face and a run of his hand through his tousled hair he stepped through the door to fetch an armload of firewood. Splitting one piece into kindling with the axe, he loaded up and walked back into the bunkhouse, dropped the wood with a clatter and opened the door with a creak of the hinge and began the work of starting the fire. All of his noise was met with complaints and groans from the nearby bunk mates and one even threw a boot his direction which he deftly ducked and continued with his work. As the kindling flamed up, he stuffed the split wood into the small door of the stove, opened the hamper and shut the door. The roar of the fire sounded its way up the chimney and the heat began to spread to the comfort of the slower rising ranch hands.

The three McPherson brothers were easily picked out by their curly red hair and the oldest, Patrick, sported a bit of a beard. All the men slowly rolled to the sides of their bunks and started their morning routine of dressing and making the trip to the privy, and soon the clanging of the striker against the triangle of the dinner bell told of the waiting fare in the chow shack. The seven men lined up at the food table and filled their plates before making their way to the long table and benches. Skinny, J.W. and the two hands named Jake and Monty were seated along one side and faced the three brothers and Hoppy, the ramrod. Shamus spoke up and asked J.W., "So where ya come from feller?"

J.W. looked up to see if the speaker was addressing him and as all the men on that side of the table were looking at him he guessed right in assuming he was the subject of the question and responded, "Well, most recently I came from the mountains South West of Ft. Laramie where I spent some time with the Utes, but 'fore that I was on a wagon train from Missouri with my folks."

Patrick piped in with, "Oh great, an Injun lover, that's just what we need around here."

J.W. wisely ignored the remark and continued putting away the biscuits and gravy in anticipation of a long day.

Shamus continued with his questioning, "Ft. Laramie, huh? Ain't that way up North a spell?"

"It's the main fort just outta Nebraska territory on the Emigrant or Oregon trail where most trains stop to resupply."

"Well, ifn' you was with yore folks an' headin' for Oregon, why'd ya quit?"

"My folks both passed, Pa from Injuns and Ma from sickness, so I just headed out to someplace warmer," he answered continuing to clean up his plate.

Patrick again interjected, "So yore Pa was killed by Injuns and you still lived with 'em? If that don't beat all!"

Looking at the older brother and giving him the once over to see if he was picking a fight or just expressing an opinion,

J.W. answered, "The Injuns that killed Pa were Pawnee and they don't like any white man. The Ute that I visited for a while were in the Rockies and usually aren't too friendly with whites, but an old chief invited me to come learn a little bit about the Indians and the mountains and I did. And I'm glad I did, they're a good people. You see, my friend, just like everybody sittin' at this table is different, think different, live different and believe different, it's the same with Indians. There are some good 'uns and some bad 'uns. But I believe God wants us to give everybody a chance and not to judge anyone before we really know them."

"Oh great, just what we need, a Bible thumper! So now you're gonna start preachin' to us?"

"No, I just told you what I believe about people, all people that's all. Take it however you want," replied J.W. as he wiped his plate with the last piece of biscuit, emptied his coffee cup and stood up to leave the table. Patrick grumbled to his plate and continued his eating and fussing with anything that seemed to irk him, which was just about everything. J.W. walked from the cook shack to the corral and putting his foot on the bottom rail, rested his arms on the top rail and looked over the herd of horses. Horses, like most animals, when in a group will seek to find the dominant one or become the dominant one. He watched as they moved around and noticed his steel dust gelding had assumed a leadership position as the others yielded to him at the hay pile. Although mild mannered with J.W., his horse was well muscled and at sixteen hands was a bit taller than the average. J.W. had recently begun calling him Smoke and now J.W. whistled and said, "Come 'ere Smoke ol boy." The gelding lifted his head at the whistle and stood still as he looked to his owner, then bobbing his head up and down and with his tail raised high he pranced to the fence to nuzzle his master. J.W. scratched the head and nose of the horse and talked to him all the while, and reaching through the top two rails, he patted the horse's neck and scratched behind his ears, to the enjoyment of the animal.

38

"That's a mighty fine looking animal ya got there," came a voice from behind him. J.W. turned to see the bowlegged Hoppy approaching. Hoppy was a Tom look-alike except for the bowed legs and the drooping handle bar mustache. With graying hair, weathered wrinkles on his sun browned skin, the man was a little shorter than J.W. but his shoulders and chest showed a man that could work and fight most others to a standstill. Like Tom of the Spear V, Hoppy wore gambler stripped britches tucked into the high tops of the Mexican boots and held up by suspenders that now supported the thumbs of the ramrod. Taking a similar stance at the fence, the foreman said, "Don't let Patrick get under yore skin, he does that with ever'body. I think he's tryin' to prove to his ol' man that he's just as big as he is, but he's got a long ways ta go to measure up to ol' man McPherson. However, they are cut from the same cloth, I reckon. But gittin' in a tussle with him won't do you much good. Ifn' ya' beat him, the ol' man'll probly run ya' off, and if'n you lose, then ya' won't be able ta' git him to shut up 'bout it an' you'll probly wanna leave anyhow. "

"I understand; I've run into fellas like him before. Wherever ya go, there's a bully or a wannabe that's out to prove hisself. Ain't no way to live, in my book," answered J.W.

"Well, I'm right proud ta' hear ya say that, son. Well, anyway, fer today, I wantcha to muck out them stalls in the barn yonder. The boss an' his daughter, Florence, keep thar horses in there an' they like ta' spoil 'em so keep them stalls mucked out. After ya do that, get a sack o' lye outta the shed yonder and pitch a scoop 'er two down the privies and make sure there's some o' them ol newspapers or catalogs in 'em. After ya' get done with that, ya need ta' pitch some hay to the hosses, both them in the barn and them in the corral and make shore they all gots water. I'll be back round 'bout noon and check on ya' and give ya' some more chores to do. Think ya' can handle all that, do ya?"

"Easy 'nuff, but say, Hoppy, how long ya figger it'll be 'fore I can get to doin' some real work, with cattle I mean?"

"Oh, that'll come soon 'nuff. Them cows are startin' ta drop their calves and the rest of us'll be playin' midwife. After a few days we'll need ever' hand we got helpin' them mommas with their youngun's or helpin' them young'uns ta' git here. After that, we'll need ta' keep 'em paired up and make shore they's nursin' o.k. and if not, we gotta pair 'em up with a momma that'll take care'o more'n one, or maybe a momma that lost hers, ya know, kinda adopt 'em out. But when that gits started, we'll need ever' man in the field, an' you'll get a go at it," reassured Hoppy.

"All right, then, guess I better get started, thanks Hoppy." Heading to the barn and his not so pleasant task, J.W. was thinking, *Boy, I didn't think about all that, that's quite a bit playin' nursemaid to a bunch of cows. I just figgered they handled that all on their own, but I guess I've got a lot to learn.*

Chapter Eight

Mucking

THREE DAYS OF MUCKING STALLS, forking hay, and throwing lime brought J.W. to a level of boredom and frustration the like of which he hadn't experienced since childhood when everything involving work was frustrating. The only break in the monotony was the extra task of repairing the adobe wall around the place, patching the peeling clay with a fresh batch of mud. As he mindlessly raked the piles of manure into a central pile, sorting the horse apples from the straw, he thought about what Hoppy said about the nurse-maiding of the cattle. "Even a messy newborn calf would be better than all this manure!" he muttered.

"Have you ever pulled a calf to know how messy it really is?" asked a voice from behind him. J.W. spun around to see the prettiest vision he ever imagined and she was smiling at him. Florence McPherson was the redhead daughter of old man McPherson and from J.W.'s point of view she appeared as if a glow of light shone about her. He was tongue tied as he tried to answer, "Uh . . .uh . . . uh, no I reckon I haven't."

"Well, the first time you have to reach in and pull one out, you'll change your tune right quick. The first time I had to do it I 'bout lost my lunch right then and there!" she exclaimed.

"You mean to tell me you've . . . you've . . . done that?" he asked incredulously.

"Why of course, silly. I'm a ranch girl and we've been doin' that ever since we got our first bunch of cows. That's part of ranchin'" she replied with a bit of a mischievous smile tugging at the corners of her lips. J.W. looked at her and was awed by what he saw. Standing with feet wide apart to show she was wearing a split skirt that touched the tops of her fancy Mexican boots, and bright green blouse with lace around the collar and topped off with a fringed vest that matched her skirt. She had a felt hat jauntily cocked to the side that did little to shade her green eyes and the broad smile that stretched her freckled face. J.W. thought she was the prettiest girl he had ever seen. He stood and stared wordlessly as he leaned on the muck rake.

"Uh, if you're not going to use that rake, how 'bout saddlin' up my mare for me?" asked the redhead.

"Uh, sure! Be glad to!" proclaimed an eager J.W.

He led the palomino mare out of the stall and tethered her to the gatepost. He turned to go to the tack shed for her gear and almost bumped into her as she struggled with her saddle, bridle and blanket. He took it from her and within moments had the mare saddled and ready to go and led her out of the barn to hold her for the girl to mount. She looked at him and smiled and asked, "Why don't you go with me? Surely you can spare an hour or so from your very important duties?"

"Uh, I don't know, Miss, I don't think Hoppy'd like me takin' off."

"Ah, he won't mind you goin' with me, after all, my Pa don't like me ridin' alone, and he'd consider it a personal favor."

He looked at the sincere expression of Florence and thought a moment then answered, "Well, since you put it that way, it probably would be best if you didn't ride out alone. Ya' never know what might happen to a girl out there by herself. I'll get my gear and be ready in a minute." J.W. trotted to the tack shed for his gear as Florence watched his retreat she smiled and thought, *Little does he know I've been riding this ranch by myself since I was twelve.*

Their leisurely ride took them across the grassy plains toward the rocky juniper littered bluffs where J.W. first stopped to look over what would be his new temporary home. Florence chattered all the way and J.W. listened and learned. Just by watching her he knew she was an excellent horsewoman, confident and commanding of her mount, but also a sensitive girl as she often spoke encouragement and affection to the palomino. She called her horse by name, Blondie, and often reached down to stroke her neck and run her fingers through her mane. Florence talked about her brothers and it was evident her favorite was Sean, the quiet one who was happy all the time and friendly with everyone. She also spoke of Shamus and his easy going way and how he was such a committed Christian and read his Bible regularly. There was nothing said of Patrick. Florence looked at her companion and asked, "J.W. are you a Christian?" He was surprised at her directness in asking the question but he answered, "Why, is that important to you?"

"Yes, it is, and it should be important to you too. If you're not a Christian, life would be without purpose and hopeless. I didn't realize how hopeless until I accepted Christ as my Savior and discovered how wonderful it is to have that hope of eternal life in Heaven with Him." Turning to look directly at J.W. she asked again, "Well, are you?"

J.W. reined his mount to a nearby juniper, dropped down to the ground and tethered his horse to the tree, reached for the reins and lead rope of the palomino and tethered the mare beside his steel dust and helped Florence to the ground. He motioned for her to follow him to the promontory and said for her to join him on the large boulder. Making themselves as comfortable as possible, they looked across the wide expanse of green meadow and J.W. began to tell the story of his life before he came to Texas.

He told how his father explained to him God's simple plan of salvation, how everyone is a sinner and the penalty for sin is death, but that Christ paid that penalty on the cross of Calvary and purchased the free gift of salvation, the gift that had to be accepted by those that chose to believe. He shared how as a young teenager he knelt by the side of his bed alongside his father and prayed to receive that gift. "After that, my life changed, but so did Pa's. He felt God calling him to become a pastor and then a missionary to the pioneers and Indians. That's how come we were on the wagon train when Pa was killed and Ma died later. So, after that I just headed South and here I am."

"I'm glad you're here," replied Florence as she shyly bowed her head and looked at her hands.

"Me too," said J.W. as he reached over to take her hand in his.

She looked up at him and smiled and said, "Say, you can come to church with us tomorrow! There's a nice little church in town and the pastor's a good man, you'll like him!" she proclaimed excitedly.

"Sure, that'd be great! I'd like to go to church with you, it's been a while since I've been in a real church. But for right now, we better be gettin' back 'fore somebody thinks we got lost."

Back at the ranch, J.W. had tethered his horse by the corral and followed Florence as she rode Blondie into the barn. He gave her a hand as she dismounted and took the lead rope from her saying, "I'll put her up for you Miss Florence."

"I told you, it's not Miss Florence, just plain Florence or Flo if you'd like."

"Yeah, I'd like that a lot . . . Flo," he answered with a bashful head down smile. She reached out and grabbed his hand, gave it a squeeze and said, "Now don't forget about tomorrow! You're coming to church with us, y'hear?"

"I won't forget, I'm lookin' forward to it," he answered, grinning.

After putting up her horse, he returned to his duties with the muck rake and started whistling. The rest of the day was spent on his mindless chores but his mind was on other things, or people, as he whistled his way through the remainder of the day. When Hoppy returned with Sean and Shamus, they noticed the smile on J.W.'s face and the glazed look in his eyes and quickly guessed the cause to be their winsome sister. As they unsaddled and turned their horses into the corral, they looked at J.W., shook their heads and Sean said to Shamus, "Looks like our sister has bagged herself a duck!" Shamus smiled and nodded in agreement as they made their way to the bunkhouse. When Patrick came in Shamus said to his brother, "Did you see that look on the new hand's face?"

"Whatdaya mean? I ain't even looked at him."

"I think he's smitten with our sister," informed Shamus.

"He better not be! I'll have to pound some sense into that feller's head. If he knows what's good for him, he'll stay shy of her!" threatened the big brother.

"But whatcha gonna do 'bout Flo if she comes around lookin' fer him?" asked Sean.

"We'll straighten her out. Just like that last one that came out here from town, didn't take long for him to see the error of his ways."

Sean and Shamus just shook their heads knowing the temper of their big brother and the way he thought he was the protector of their sister. They had often discussed what it would be like to have an old maid for a sister since Patrick was certain no man was good enough for her. Maybe this'n be different, they agreed.

Chapter Nine

Church

A STRAWBERRY ROAN was teamed with a dark blue roan to pull the buckboard that carried Ian and Rebecca McPherson and Florence. The girl had spread a patch work quilt across a rigged bench seat behind her parents upon which she sat proudly arrayed in her blue gingham and lace trimmed dress. A white parasol rested on her shoulder as she smiled at J.W. as he rode alongside the buckboard on his long legged steel dust gelding. Ian, apparently in a foul mood, ignored the young man that was talking to his daughter and laughing at her comments about the day and the journey. The road was dry and dusty and the three brothers that obediently followed the buckboard were choking on the dust stirred up by the team and wagon. The family tradition was to attend the little church known as Bell's Chapel in the nearby village and afterwards get the mercantile owner to fill their weekly supply list before returning home. The village was just over an hour's ride from the ranch and it was not the patriarch's practice to waste the time on a separate trip. He tolerated the church service, believing he had no need for a sermon from some snot-nosed kid that thought he was something that he wasn't, but he thought the boys needed all the guidance they could get so he acceded to his wife's wishes. The bluster of the old man didn't hide the fact from anyone that Rebecca Jane McPherson knew how to handle her red bearded bully of a husband that ruled the roost of the McPherson spread.

The building had rough cut lap board siding, two windows per side, and a single door that welcomed the Sunday morning worshippers. The church stood alone at the end of the short main street of the village that would one day become the town of Italy, so named by the mercantile owner that always wanted to visit Europe. The village consisted of the mercantile store, one false-fronted canvas saloon and about a half dozen adobe dwellings that were in various states of disrepair. The church was founded by the pastor, Jacob Bell, the brother of one of the ranchers in the area, and this was his first experience at leading a church. A studious young man, he sought to make his sermons practical and applicable to the daily life of the members of the community, but he occasionally found himself expounding on some recently discovered theological truth that elicited glazed stares from his congregation. He meant well, but his inexperience with life's many lessons branded some of his sermons with hypocrisy. As was typical of the solitary churches in communities of the time, the gathering at church by all the ranchers and others from the far-flung settlement was as much a social time as it was spiritual. Families would arrive early, enjoy the service of singing and sharing, and then gather together outside for a community meal set on the planks and sawhorses and surrounded by the benches carried out from the church. Behind the church building was a long lean-to where folks stabled their horses and parked their wagons and buggies. The activities around the church were usually an all-day outing for everyone.

As the crowd made their way into the small church, it was apparent there were not enough benches for everyone. Lining the back of the large room, several cowboys and vaqueros stood holding their hats with hands clasped in front of them.

J.W. and the brothers joined the standing men while James Enoch, Rebecca and Florence took their customary place on the second bench from the front. Within moments the church was full and the visiting subsided as the pastor took his place behind the pulpit. He lifted his hands and began leading the singing of The Lily of the Valley.

I have found a friend in Jesus, He's everything to me,
He's the fairest of ten thousand to my soul.
The Lily of the Valley in Him alone I see,
All I need to cleanse and make me fully whole.

After several more songs, the pastor began his sermon by reading his text from Romans 10:9 *That if thou shalt confess with thy mouth the Lord Jesus, and shalt believe in thine heart that God hath raised him from the dead, thou shalt be saved.*

He expounded on the difference between saying you believe in God and really believing in your heart and taking Him by faith. He concluded with a brief invitation for people to bow their heads and if they knew for sure that Heaven was their home, to raise their hands. Most present raised their hands but many of the men standing at the back just shuffled their feet in impatience while J.W. alone raised his hand to proclaim his faith in Christ. The pastor encouraged all to examine their hearts and if they wanted to be sure of Heaven, to feel free to talk with him afterwards. He closed with prayer and asked the men at the back to assist in carrying out the benches for the anticipated dinner that followed. As the crowd pushed its way out the door, the pastor stood on the small stoop and shook hands with all the adults then stepped aside as the men carried out the benches and began setting up the plank tables.

The church grounds were soon littered with clusters of people seated on blankets and visiting over the plates of shared food. Cowboys found girlfriends, older children were grouped near the swings, one cluster was made up of widow ladies while another was weathered old ranchers with both groups sneaking looks and smiles at the other. J.W. had seated himself at the end of the buckboard and was trying to balance his plate on his lap when Florence asked him to scoot over and make room for her. He gladly complied by stepping down and helping her up by lifting her at the waist and seating her on the edge of the buckboard's plank box. "Why, you're as light as a feather!" he proclaimed with a broad smile.

"What'd you expect, a sack of oats?" she retorted.

"Uh, no, no, that's not what I meant at all. I was just sayin' . . . uh . . ." he stammered and she rescued the embarrassed J.W. when she replied with, "I know, I was just funnin' you. Come on and sit back down so's we can visit," she instructed.

After a short while of visiting about the church, the service and other 'make talk' topics, the couple looked up to see the pastor approaching with an enthusiastic grin and an outstretched hand. "Hello again, Florence, is this the young man you were telling me about?" he asked.

"Yes pastor, this is J.W. Harpold. J.W., this is pastor Jacob Bell."

"Pleased to meet you, Pastor," said J.W. as he started to step down from the buckboard but was stopped by the upraised hand of the young pastor.

"Likewise, J.W. Say, if you've got a minute, I'd like to ask a question, if you don't mind?"

"Go right ahead," replied J.W.

"Well, Florence shared with me that your father was a pastor, is that right?"

"Yessir, but he was killed before he could follow what he thought the Lord wanted him to do, to try to minister to the pioneers and the Indians," explained J.W.

"That's too bad, but what I wanted to talk about was more about you. Did you do any teaching with your father or the church or anything?"

"Yessir, of course it seems like I was either being schooled or doing the schooling almost all my life. I helped start the Sunday School at the last church in Missouri before we started out West. We had about a dozen students of all ages."

49

"Great! That's great! That's just what we need here. There are several families with young children, maybe ten or twelve or so, but there is no other school around for them. Tell me more about the Sunday School you had in Missouri," asked the pastor.

"Well, it was kinda like here. We'd have church service, then dinner on the grounds, and after that the children would go into the building and we'd have school for about three or four hours. Taught everything from reading to arithmetic and more, course our main book was the Bible. Sometimes, some of the parents would sit in and try to learn themselves, but it was all very good and I enjoyed the teaching."

The pastor was rubbing his hands together and shifting his weight from one foot to the other in his eagerness, nodding his head in agreement and excitement with what J.W. was saying and when J.W. paused, he interjected, "Do you think you could do something like that here? We've got the students and I have two sets of the new McGuffey readers that you could use to help teach the reading. Would you consider it, please?" he pleaded. Florence was smiling and nodding as she looked from J.W. to the pastor.

J.W. looked at the pastor who appeared to be about the same age, maybe younger, and considered what he'd been asked. "Well, my first responsibility is to Mr. McPherson, and I'd have to clear it with him, but I'd like to give it some thought and get back with you. Say, by next Sunday?"

Florence spoke up and said, "I'd help you, J.W.! I think it would be great for the kids and the families too. They haven't had the opportunity for any kind of education and it could be the best thing for everyone!" she declared enthusiastically. J.W. smiled at her and thought, *that would be a way to spend more time with her and without her old man looking over my shoulder.*

"Well, let's see what your Pa has to say about it."

"That won't be a problem. I'll just tell Ma and she'll handle him!"

50

Chapter Ten

Vaquero

HOPPY'S BIG BOOT at the end of J.W.'s bunk jarred the sleepyhead from his slumber. He cracked open one eye to the darkness and quickly looked at the foot of his bed to see the shadowed image of the ramrod about to kick his bunk again. "Come on ol' son, time ta' rise n' shine! We're burnin' daylight."

J.W. sat up, stretched and yawned and asked, "What daylight? The sun's still asleep, like I should be. What's so important 'bout muckin' out stalls that they can't wait a couple hours?"

"You ain't muckin' today. We got us a new hand, or an old hand that returned, an' I want you ta go out with him this mornin', so get your lazy rump outta bed an' git ya' some grits an' git a move on," ordered the ramrod as he moved on to the next occupied bunk.

J.W. put on his hat, dropped his feet over the edge of his bunk and pulled on his trousers, stomped his feet into his boots and slipped his shirt over his head and tucked in the tail and stretched his suspenders over his shoulders. Walking to the cook shack he was joined by the vaquero who introduced himself, "I am Alvar Jose Antonio Cabeza deVaca, and you?"

"I'm J.W. Harpold," answered J.W. extending his hand to shake with Alvar.

"Ah, Si, Senor Hoppy said we'd be working together. He told me to 'show you the ropes' and to see if I can make a cowboy out of you. What you theenk, will you make a cowboy?"

"I think so," replied J.W. as he looked at the vaquero. Alvar was easily eight or ten years his senior and his attire showed the purpose for which it was fashioned. Close fitting trousers with leather along the inside of the legs that flared over the tops of hand crafted boots that sported big roweled spurs. His short jacket was open to a white big collared shirt and his face was shaded by the sombrero favored by the vaqueros.

"I have been doing thees a long time, senor, and I can teach you ever'theeng you need to know. I'm a very good teacher," he reassured J.W. and patted his new friend on the shoulder.

After a quick breakfast, the two new partners returned to the corral and set about gearing up for the day. Alvar noticed the riata on J.W.'s saddle and complimented him for having the judgment of having a rawhide riata rather than the new woven ropes that many of the cowboys favored. "The riata is mucho strong compared to the ropes of the others. It will keep its loop farther and will last longer," he explained.

"Well, I got it from a couple friends of mine I traveled with for a while. They showed me some of the basics, but I could use a lotta help, that's fer sure," replied J.W.

Hoppy had instructed the pair to head out to the North East pasture and sort out and bring in the heavies. Heavies were the cows that appeared ready to drop their calves. Many of the mother cows had calved, but sometimes the younger cows had a more difficult time of birthing and the rancher preferred to have them closer so if help was needed, it would be available. Alvar explained the quickest way to identify the heavies was the size of their belly and if they were 'bagging up' or if their udder was swollen and ready to feed a new calf. The North East pasture held somewhere between four and five hundred cows and the task of sorting them out began immediately. Alvar instructed his protégé to follow his lead as they rode around the outside edges of the herd. This pasture was mostly open grassland with few obstacles or thickets and the work of the day began easily enough. Whenever a heavy was spotted, they would slowly work between the cow and the rest of the herd, move it away toward the lower end of the pasture and keep any others from following. As the two separated the first couple of cows, the mothers to be moved away and trotted with bouncing bellies in front of the horses. J.W. continued to drive the two as Alvar returned to the herd. J.W. had been instructed to stay with the cows until Alvar was able to bring some more so the first couple would settle down and not try to return to the herd. The first couple of hours passed easily and it seemed to J.W. this job was easier than he expected until an old mossy horned brindle cow that hung around the only thicket of brush decided she didn't want to do what the cowboys expected. Every time one of them would approach the wild eyed cow, she would lower her head and charge the horse swinging her head side to side in an attempt to gore the offending animal. After several unsuccessful tries, Alvar said, "When I tell you, you move to the cow and keep her attention. I weel come from behind and drop a loop over her head and we'll try to drag her to the others." Alvar spurred his mount, a tall long maned black gelding, toward the back side of the thicket. Pushing his way through the brush, the vaquero came clear and with one quick swing over his head he dropped the wide loop over the horns of the surprised cow that tossed her head and sought escape. Before she could move two steps, the vaquero had dallied his riata around the big horn of his Mex saddle and turned his mount to the side to jerk the cow away from J.W. He hollered at J.W. "Drop a loop over her head and we can take her!"

Fumbling with his riata, he built a loop and began to swing it over his head as Alvar continued to drag the cow against her will. J.W. followed, tossed his loop, missed and pulled in his riata and started building another loop. Again he swung his loop over his head one time, let loose and luckily the loop settled over the rank cow's head. He started to pull the riata tight and Alvar yelled, "No senor, dally and turn away!" J.W. caught what he said, dallied the riata around his saddle horn and reined the grey away from the cow. Now with the cow between the two, whenever the mossy horn tried to charge one horse, the other cowboy could keep a taut rope and prevent it. Fighting all the way, the cow was finally dragged kicking and bellowing to the smaller herd of heavies. J.W. asked, "How do I get my riata back?"

"Throw slack, like thees," yelled Alvar as he demonstrated after releasing his dally. He flipped the slack of the rope and the loop held tight because of the taut rope from J.W. Seeing the vaquero flip his rope, J.W. copied his action and the loop was soon loose enough to drop around the neck of the cow, but not enough to release the animal. Alvar instructed him to let his rope drop as the vaquero flipped his loop back over the horns of the cow. The loosened rope of J.W., stepped on by the rangy cow, loosened and fell off. J.W. moved his horse closer and following the example taught him by his trail companion, Dusty, he grabbed his saddle horn with his left hand and bent low and picked up the riata without dismounting. As he was regaining his seat, he looked up to see the mossy horned cow charging his mount and before his britches hit the saddle, Alvar had spurred his big gelding to chest bump the hindquarters of the cow and turn it aside from striking the steel dust gelding.

The group of about twenty-five heavies were lazily grazing near a small swale out of sight from the rest of the herd. Alvar suggested they take their noon and give the horses some rest to which J.W. eagerly agreed. The thicket of brush that had been the hide out of the tough old cow was bordered by a pair of pecan trees under which the partners sought respite. With left over biscuits and bacon from the cook shack they kicked back on the patch of grass and watched their horses partake of their own feast of tall grass.

"So, how long have you lived around here, Alvar?" asked J.W.

"Ah, senor, my family has been in this part of the country for over three hundred years," answered the vaquero.

"Three hundred years? Lordy, I never thought any family lived that long in one place. Where bouts is your home?"

"The remainder of our estate is on the South side of the Rio Gande. Before all the conflicts between Mexico and Texas, our rancho was on both sides and covered several hundred thousand acres. But now, my family is just on the South side."

"Well, if ya' don't mind my askin', with a place that big, why are you workin' here?" asked the curious J.W.

"When Texas became a state, I wanted to see what it was like to be a part of that. My family has many sons and one more or less didn't matter, so I came here and worked for the big red headed McPherson. I've worked here, off and on, for almost five years. But they've been here much longer."

J.W., though curious to know more, knew he had already nosed into Alvar's history more than was acceptable so he let the subject drop and leaned back to tip his hat over his eyes for a quick nap. But before he closed his eyes, Alvar turned the tables on him and began to inquire about J.W.'s life before the McPherson's. J.W. complied and shared his story beginning with his family, the wagon train, and his jaunt South with the two friends, Dusty and Hank.

"So, you've seen quite a bit of this country? Why did you stop here in Texas?"

"Ah, me and the cold of the mountains ain't the best of friends. I kinda like the South and the warm weather, so far that is. But the mountains shore are pretty, I did like that about 'em. Maybe after I learn everything you're gonna teach me, I might try ranchin' my own self. I dunno, guess I'll just take what comes," he surmised. Their brief rest soon passed and the partners were back on the job of sorting out the heavies. Two more hours of sorting brought the smaller herd to a few head over fifty and Alvar said they needed to start them back to the lower pasture closer into headquarters.

After letting the small herd of heavies settle in to the lower pasture, the men headed toward the corrals but on the way Alvar chose to do a little teaching. After demonstrating building a loop and the swing of the loop, he had J.W. follow suit. Then with additional instruction, he watched J.W., gave pointers and encouragement and told the student he needed to practice, practice, practice. After unsaddling their mounts and putting up their gear, J.W. carried his riata around, building loops and throwing them to rope anything and everything from rocks to bushes to barrels and even tried for a rabbit. Every spare moment, he was seen throwing loops and practicing what Alvar had instructed. With each throw he gained more and more confidence and Alvar told him, "When we have to do a round up or to do some branding, we will need every hand to be able to do his share. Eet ees a lot of work when we have to brand many hundred cattle. When you get better, I will show you how to lay your loop down to just catch the heels of the calf, you need to know how to do that to stretch out the calf to brand heem."

Nodding to his teacher, J.W. continued to walk around the buildings throwing his loop at anything and everything. From behind him came a familiar voice, "You're looking more and more like a real cowboy!"

"I think I've got a lot a' learnin' to do before I can wear that title," answered J.W. as he turned to see Florence walking toward him.

"I wanted you to know, I talked to my mother about the Sunday School and she uh . . . explained to my father how the routine for Sunday's would change. So, if you're still willing to do it, I'm ready to help you," she said with a broad smile.

56

"It'll be a challenge, but I think it will be a good thing. There's always a reward in that kind of work, just to see the kids learning to read and such. Even the adults can make it special. Yeah, I think it'll be a good thing to do, don't you?"

"I do. I've already decided to trail my horse behind the buckboard so my folks don't have to wait for us and we can come home together after we're done teaching," she said with a mischievous glint in her eye.

J.W. caught the expression and he smiled conspiratorially and thought, *yeah, my Ma said a man chases a woman until she catches him. I'm thinkin' I might be gettin' caught.*

Chapter Eleven

Jokesters

THE BRIGHT SUN glared from the horizon as Alvar and J.W. rode to the North East pasture to finish sorting the heavies. During the casual ride, J.W. continued his practice throwing loops, coiling his riata and throwing again all with the supervision of Alvar. Occasionally the vaquero would give a pointer but overall he was pleased with the progress of his student. Most of the morning was spent using the riata as nothing more than a whip whenever some stubborn cow would insist on grabbing another bite of grass before moving out, a chest bump from the horse and a smack on the rump from the loop of the riata usually changed their mind. The sorting was going well until J.W. spotted another cow trying to hide out in the same thicket that harbored the mossy horn brindle from the day before. Without hesitating, J.W. goaded his mount into the thicket in pursuit with branches grabbing at his legs and swatting him in the face. Holding his arm in front of his face to shield his eyes, J.W. pushed his mount straight through the thicket and smack into the biggest wasp nest he ever saw. Quicker than he could say Jack Spratt, the wasps retaliated and swarmed after the attacker of their nest. In that instant J.W. spurred the steel dust and they both blew out of the thicket with J.W. swatting at the yellow and black horde around his head and yelling at the attackers as if they could understand him. Just two steps free of the thicket and the steel dust dropped his head between his front feet and tried to kick the clouds with his rear hooves. J.W.'s thighs grabbed at the swells of the pommel and he leaned back losing his hat to the whipping tail of his mount. The horse switched ends and now reared up and tried to rake the blue from the sky with his fore hooves and snatch bites from the clouds with his bared teeth. J.W. bounced off the cantle of his saddle as the horse once again dropped his head between his front hooves and rubbed the dirt with his nose. His back end twisted and the gelding tried to lose the stinging wasps from his belly with a kick. He squealed and grunted with every buck and launched himself into a high flying gut twisting sun fishing leap as the fringe of J.W.'s shotgun chaps flared in the wind. When the two came down from their attempt at flight, all four hooves landed almost simultaneously and J.W. thought he was dropping through the seat of his saddle clear to the ground. With every bone feeling the crunch he leaned over his saddle horn and buried his face in the mane of the now still and panting horse that sought to gain breath after his workout. Sitting up and looking around, J.W. rubbed his neck, felt a protruding stinger and pinched it out then repeated the process with another over his eye and on the back of his hand. Alvar, retrieving J.W.'s hat, handed it to him and rode easily alongside the heavy breathing man, smiled and said, "Ah, the wasps, they geet you, eh? Come wit' me, wee'll get some mud to put on them, it'll help."

As they rode to the swale that harbored the heavies, the steel dust kept bobbing his head and occasionally sidestepping in frustration. When they stopped near a mud hole, J.W. examined the horse and found a couple of wasps still entangled in his mane and three evident stings along the horse's neck. Removing the stingers and applying mud soothed the horse and the man as the men chose to take their noon break. "You rode heem pretty good. I thought he was going to lose you but you took a deep seat and hung on. You might make a cowboy yet, gringo!"

"After that last buck, I think I'll be a couple inches shorter the way he pounded me into that saddle," shared J.W. as he arched his back to try to remove the kinks.

"All in a day's work," surmised Alvar.

Both men stretched out on the tall grass and tipping their hats over their eyes, sought a short nap while their horses grazed contentedly nearby. Awakened by a light sprinkle of rain, they rose from their grass beds and stretched. Alvar stood to find the grazing horses and said, "Look, look! There's two white tail bucks over there. Aiiee . . . I would like some venison steak for supper, but they would be gone before we could get there. Oh well . . ."

J.W. looked in the direction his friend pointed and spotted the two deer walking broadside and snatching mouths full of grass with each pause. He looked at Alvar, then walked to his mount and withdrew the Sharps from the scabbard. Returning to the side of his curious friend, he knelt to one knee, popped up his peep sight and calculated the range, asking Alvar, "How far ya figger, three or four hundred yards?"

"Si, si, but that ees too far, it's over three hundred yards," exclaimed Alvar.

J.W. rested his left elbow on his knee, held the Sharps steady, took his aim, set the rear trigger and slowly squeezed the small front trigger. The explosion and burst of grey smoke startled the vaquero who jumped back stumbling to regain his footing, shielded his eyes and saw one buck bound away leaving his grazing partner in the grass. Alvar looked at J.W. as the young man started to rise, then looked to the downed deer and back at J.W. as he said, "That is good shooting, senor. I didn't theenk you could do that but you surprised me."

J.W. smiled and as he replaced the Sharps in the scabbard replied, "Well, there's your fresh venison steak. We better get it dressed out and get it and these heavies back to headquarters so Cooky can fix your supper."

They pushed the two dozen heavies back to the small meadow near the headquarters to join the others that busied themselves with the tall grass. The near meadow had been reserved for just this purpose and the green grass was an open invitation to the weary fat bellied cows. After dropping the dressed out deer carcass at the cook shack, the two partners busied themselves putting up the horses and gear. Alvar spoke, "Uh, my friend, I theenk I should warn you. The brothers have a habit of trying to initiate any new hands by pulling some prank on them. Just be careful, because they can be pretty mean and if you don't take it right, they are very quick to fight. Especially that Patrick, hee's always looking for an excuse to fight."

"Why, thanks Alvar. That's good to know. I figgered that about Patrick, but the other two seem to be O.K. Pranks huh? I wonder what they think they're gonna do? I'm purty good at prankin' my own self."

"Just be careful, senor, he can get pretty mean. I remember one time a couple of years ago, their prank turned into a shooting and the other cowboy got hit."

"You mean they killed a man?" asked J.W. incredulously.

"No, but he was laid up a long time and then he left the country, he said no job was worth dying for."

"Well, I agree with him on that. Thanks Alvar, I'll walk lightly and we'll just have to see what happens."

J.W. was the first one done with his supper and got up to leave wanting to shake out a loop or two to continue his practice, Alvar followed soon after. After the two partners left the cook shack, the brothers began talking with Patrick grumbling, "That greenhorn is gettin' under my skin, especially the way that vaquero was braggin' on him makin' that shot to bring down that deer. If I had me a Sharps I coulda made that shot too. He ain't so hot."

"He's provin' to be a pretty good hand. Pa thinks he might

be worth keepin' on," commented Shamus.

"Ah . . . he ain't nuthin' special. I think we need to do a little initiatin' on him, see what kinda man he really is," stated Patrick.

Sean piped in, "Ah he ain't so bad. You don't want him to get outta sorts like that fella did that you shot. Pa won't like that."

"I ain't worried about Pa. We ain't gonna do no shootin' anyhow. I got a better idea, we'll take care of him after he turns in tonight," ordered Patrick.

As J.W. strolled the grounds around the buildings he continued working with his riata, building a loop, throwing it at whatever was handy and repeating. Alvar told him the riata had to become a natural extension of his arm so much so that whatever he looked at he could lasso. The initial swelling from the wasp bites had gone down but he still smarted from the stings and stopping by the water trough, he dipped his hand for a scoop of water to cool his forehead and neck. "Boy, those wasps really did you turn, didn't they?" asked Florence as she walked to his side. J.W. looked up and smiled at the vision he had thought about all day and answered, "Yeah, they did. I ain't never seen so many of them things all at onct in my life!"

"Uh, if you're going to be a School teacher, maybe you better start working on your language. You know, ain't and onct aren't exactly the words you need to teach the students."

With a chuckle he answered, "No, but it's pretty easy to fall into the common vernacular of the area and the people you're around."

She smiled back at him and said, "I think you're going to do just fine! I'm certain the children and even the adults will be great students. I'm excited about helping."

J.W. and Florence began to walk side by side as J.W. continued his practice and Florence continuing her chit chat of thoughts and anticipations. Patrick exited the cook shack as the two walked between the barn and tack sheds and he shook his head at the sight thinking *He ain't good 'nuff for her, we'll have to put a stop to that and I'm thinkin' Pa would agree.*

The morning sun had yet to make an appearance when the men in the bunkhouse started stirring to start a new day. The only light came from a single candle at the far end away from the door. J.W. stirred to some degree of wakefulness, grabbed his hat from the corner post of his bunk and thinking of the urgency of a trip to the privy, threw his legs over the edge of the bunk, grabbed his britches from the foot of the bed and started to slip them on, he started to stand and scooted off the edge only to plummet through empty space and land on his face on the floor. With pants around his ankles, he got to his knees amidst the roaring laughter of all the men in the bunkhouse. The brothers had done their deed in the night when they lifted his bunk while he slept and placed the legs on pieces of firewood making the edge of the bunk about four feet off the floor.

J.W. stood, pulled up his britches and stretched the suspenders over his shoulders, stomped his feet into his boots and as the laughter subsided, he looked at the smiling co-conspirators and said, "Well played fellas, but just remember, what goes around, comes around." J.W. turned to the door and with the sun peeking over the distant horizon, made his way to the privy and began plotting his revenge.

Chapter Twelve

Sunday School

JACOB BELL, THE PASTOR of Bell's chapel, had a vision and burden for the community long before he began the church. The younger brother of Jackson Bell and the second son of Jeremiah and Eliza Bell, Jacob never showed any interest in the ranch and the accompanying struggles and trials of the family throughout the conflicts with Mexico, Indians and the weather. These things only succeeded in driving Jacob deeper into his studies of God's Word. At the tender age of eight, Jacob told his mother he wanted to be a preacher but little did she know that her son felt he was such a sinner at that youthful age that his only chance at Heaven was if he surrendered to be a preacher of the Gospel.

When he turned sixteen, his mother implored his father to send young Jacob back East to attend a school for pastors. Yale Theological Seminary welcomed the young student and he quickly excelled at his studies, but soon tired of the ritual and routine and left before graduating. Yale was the principal training school for Congregationalist ministers but Jacob sought no support or acknowledgement from the denomination and instead wanted a completely independent congregation. He started Bell's Chapel soon after his return and his vision was not just for a church but a school for the children as well. From the outset his preparations included plans for the school and he was now able to see that vision come to fruition.

The usual tidbits of gossip and news that were shared at the last community gathering at the church on the previous Sunday included the speculation about a possible school. Although everyone knew the church and pastor were primarily supported by the Bell family ranch, they knew even with that support the community could not afford a full time pastor nor a full time teacher. But the people were still hopeful that something could be done to have a school for their youngsters. A community that is mostly made up of men and women that received little or no schooling in their childhood was a community that treasured the dream and possibility of an education for their children.

It was a busy week for Pastor Jacob Bell and his wife Olivia. There was much to be done to prepare for the opening of their Sunday School. When folks began arriving for the Sunday morning services, the ladies were all atwitter at the changes in the church. All the windows sported new curtains that were light and bright and lacy. Between the two windows on the East side another set of curtains were pulled together but there was no window behind them. Two taller benches were pushed against the West side and brought curious looks because they were too tall for anyone to sit on. The pastor stationed his wife in front of the center curtains to keep prying eyes from peeking and after everyone was seated, except for the usual line of cowboys standing at the back wall, the pastor began the services with the usual hymn singing. After the concluding prayer, the pastor finally answered the piqued but unasked questions with an announcement, "And finally folks," he said from behind a spreading grin, "what you've all been wondering about," he motioned to his wife that had resumed her position at the center curtain and as she drew the curtains

back to reveal, "the slate blackboard for our school!" The
gasps and applause thrilled the secret revealing pastor and he
continued, ". . .and starting right after our dinner on the
grounds, class will commence with J.W. Harpold and Florence
McPherson as the instructors." Exclamations of surprise and
excitement erupted amidst rousing applause as the crowd
turned and sought out J.W. and Florence.

Everyone was anxious for school to start and quickly
finished their meal so the men could replace the benches within
the church. Pastor Bell explained how to arrange the benches
and how the taller benches would serve as a desktop for the
students. With preparations finished, Florence gladly accepted
the small bell from the pastor and went to the front stoop to
summon the children. Six excited children rushed for the door
and one older boy followed his mother who held tightly to his
ear. J.W. directed the three boys to sit to his right and the four
girls to be seated to his left. Both benches and desktops faced
the slate blackboard behind the teacher. As J.W. began to
explain the schedule and routine of the school day, Florence
handed out the personal framed slates to the students. Excited
faces were painted with smiles on all but the oldest student,
Josiah Bell, the twelve-year-old youngest son of the Bell ranch
family and the nephew of Jacob Bell. As the instruction began,
a beaming pastor and his wife quietly exited from behind the
students and left the school to the new teachers.

J.W. used the chalk and printed his name across the top of
the slate blackboard and directly underneath wrote Florence's
name. He turned to the students and asked if anyone could
read the words on the board. Olivia Thornton, the ten-year-old
daughter of Abel and Gertrude Thornton, the owners of the
mercantile, raised her hand and timidly said, "I can try!" Then
quickly began to sound out the letters and stumbled a little over
the names but soon recognized them as the names of the
teachers and proudly pronounced both names. J.W. could tell
she didn't really read them as much as guess, but it was a start.
He accomplished what he was going for and that was to get an

initial idea as to the level of learning that each of the students held.

As previously agreed, Florence took the younger students, four in all, and went to the other side of the church as J.W. hustled the three older, two girls and the one boy, together for their instruction. Of Florence's four students two were seven-year-old girls, Grace Newton, the freckle faced redhead daughter of Amelia and Gabriel Newton, local farmers, and Elizabeth Carpenter, the daughter of the only black couple in the area, Lucas and Cinda Carpenter, the only blacksmith in the community and his wife, the only midwife. She was also blessed with twin boys, Dan Russell and Don Raymond Rundle, six-year-old tow heads from the Carl Rundle ranch.

Along with Josiah Bell and Olivia Thornton, J.W. also had Gabriella Ortega, the eight-year-old daughter of the wealthy and oldest Mexican family in the area. Their ranch was the largest in the community due to the old Spanish land grant bequeathed to the Ortegas.

Using the individual slates, Florence began with the alphabet and the sounds of each letter. With the McGuffey Primer as her guide, she worked with each student to sound out the letters and form them on the slate. The eager students followed her lead and were thrilled with each new discovery. By the end of the afternoon, each student was recognizing sounds and letters and even a few single syllable words. Florence was relieved at the simplicity of the McGuffey primer and excited about the progress of her students.

J.W. was also pleased with the first day's progress of his students. He used the McGuffey First Reader, but mostly drilled the older students on the alphabet and worked with each one and the writing of their names and single syllable words. He easily assessed that Gabriella was the quickest to learn, Josiah was smart but not very willing, and Olivia thought she knew more than she really did, but J.W. saw each one as a challenge and he was excited at the possibilities of each student.

The time swiftly passed and soon it was time to bring the first day of school to a close. J.W. dismissed the class with a short prayer and encouraged the students to take their slates home and practice what they learned. The chatter and laughter from the school kids brought smiles to both Florence and J.W. as they watched the kids leave the church. J.W. started putting the benches back in place for the next week's service and Florence pulled the curtains on the blackboard. Both had enjoyed the day with the students and were contemplating what had transpired when Patrick stomped through the door and announced to Florence, "Come on girl, I'm takin' you home!"

"But I brought my horse, I don't need you to take me home! I can ride with J.W.!"

"You ain't ridin' with no greenhorn as long as I'm here, 'sides, Pa said I should come gitcha. Now come on!" he demanded.

Florence looked at J.W. with pleading in her eyes but he shrugged his shoulders and said, "If your Pa said for him to do it, you probably oughta. I'll see you back at the ranch."

Florence's disappointment showed as she dropped her shoulders, grabbed her shawl and walked out of the church. J.W. doubted that James Enoch McPherson had told Patrick to come get his daughter but there would be no arguing with Patrick without causing quite a ruckus. If Patrick was acting on his own, J.W. was certain Florence and her mother would sort it out. For several days, J.W. had been looking forward to the expected time together on the ride back to the ranch, but such was not to be, for now, all he could do was fetch his horse and ride on out by himself.

He walked Smoke, his big steeldust gelding, into the barn, dropped down and removed the saddle and bridle and began to rub him down with a broad brush while the horse buried his face in the bucket with oats. With a halter on Smoke, J.W. led him back out to the corral, let him loose and stood at the fence with one foot on the bottom rail and watched the big grey mix with the other horses. True to her habit of sneaking up behind him, Florence spoke with a hint of anger and said, "I knew it! Pa didn't send Patrick, that was all his idea! If I was a man I'd pound him into the ground so the only company he'd have were the other worms. He would sure fit in down there!"

"Sorry Flo, but you understand if I'da done anything and your Pa really had sent him, I'da got both of us into a bunch of trouble, and I shore didn't want to get you into any trouble with your Pa. He's been a little touchy lately anyway. Does he have a problem with me bein' around you?"

With arms across her chest she stomped her feet and said, "All of 'em, Pa included, don't think anybody's good enough! If they have their way, I'll be an old maid and still living here!"

J.W. just stared at the flamboyant display and leaned back a little as if he'd catch fire in the flames of her anger. When she saw his reaction, she started giggling and said, "I'm sorry J.W., it's not your problem. That's what I get for being the only girl in the family. Brothers!"

J.W. looked down at the ground, shuffled his feet and looked back up at the girl and said, "They may be hard to deal with, but at least you've got family. You should be thankful for that."

Florence looked at the man before her and realized he was all alone. "I'm sorry J.W., I guess I am a little ungrateful. I forgot you didn't have any brothers or sisters."

"I had a sister . . . once."

"You did? Tell me about her."

"Ain't much to tell, she was just a little tyke. Her name was Mineola," he started with a bit of water welling up in his eyes, ". . . there was just Ma and Pa and me and Mini, she was a babe in the basket, and the milk cow got outta the barn cuz I left the door open. When Pa saw her takin' off down the road, he hollered and I took off and Ma sat the baby down on the floor in the basket and she took off to help get the cow. But while we was gone, just a short while, some sparks jumped out from the fireplace and caught the basket afire and the baby and most of the house burned up." He dropped his head as the tears streamed down his cheeks to drop to the ground. Florence reached out and put her hand on his arm and said, "Oh, J.W., I'm so sorry. That must have been tough on you. How old were you?"

"I'd just turned seven. Ma and Pa never said nothin' 'bout it. But I knew it was my fault. If I'd only shut the door to the barn, it wouldna happened." The simple statement revealed a burden he carried since childhood. Fire had been his terror ever since. The thought of anyone being burned alive often brought nightmares to the broad shouldered man that didn't seem to have any weakness, but now Florence knew he carried a heavy load. There was nothing she could say he hadn't already heard, but she lightly stroked his arm and said, "I'm sure God has forgiven you even though we both know it wasn't your fault. But with God's grace, we can make it through any trial, even a trial by fire. Don't you agree?"

"Yeah, I guess so. I know what you say is true, but it still hurts and . . ." without continuing he turned back to the horses and leaned on the fence. Florence stood beside him, put her arm through his and leaning against him said, "I don't care what Pa or my brothers think, I like you." He smiled, squeezed her arm and placed his big hand over her tiny fingers and said, "I kinda like you too."

Chapter Thirteen

Calving

HOPPY WALKED AROUND the table assigning the daily chores as the men enjoyed their breakfast of biscuits, gravy, grits, bacon and eggs. The McPhersons believed in feeding their men well and with a long day before them, the workers didn't hesitate to fill up. As Hoppy stood behind and between J.W. and Alvar, he put a hand on their shoulders and said, "You two are to stay in this close in pasture where the heavies are, I want you to play mid-wife to them cows. There's quite a few of 'em that're first time mommas and they might need some help gettin' the job done. So, Alvar, I 'spect you to teach the younker here the facts of life, an' Miss Flo might be out there givin' ya'll a hand at understandin' the female side o' things. So be on yore best behavior, unnerstan?" Both men nodded their understanding as they continued stuffing themselves with breakfast.

Pulling calves was not the favorite part of cowboying of any man, but all knew its necessity. Any job that couldn't be done from the back of a horse was looked down upon by most, but birthing and branding required a hands on approach and were integral parts of the ranch life. With breakfast behind them, the two cowhands set about preparing for the day by catching their horses and saddling up. As J.W. pulled the latigo on his saddle, he asked Alvar, "Say, didn't Hoppy say somethin' 'bout Miss Flo comin' out there with us?"

Alvar looked at his saddle companion and smiled and replied, "Now you know he deed, who you trying to keed? You've been looking over your shoulder for her ever since we came out here."

"Well, I was just wonderin' if we should saddle up that palomino for her. Seems like that'd be the right thing to do, don't you think?"

"Si, but we don' know how soon she be coming, and if we saddle her horse and she has to stand half the day, not a good theeng. Besides, she has been saddling her horse since shee was a leetle girl. She can do it O.K."

With another look over his shoulder toward the main house, J.W. finished tightening the cinch, checked the back cinch and stepped aboard Smoke. Oftentimes ranch horses are a little skittish first thing in the morning and fresh under saddle and would often test the resolve of their riders by a few crowhops across the flat, but Smoke and J.W. had an understanding that was no way to begin a long hard day and the horse should save his energies for the day's work. Shifting his weight from side to side, feeling the familiar friend beneath him and the creak of the leather that was pleasing to his ears, J.W. took a deep whiff of the morning air that was laced with the smell of leather, horses, and a hint of the fresh fragrance of the blue bonnets in the valley, he smiled, ready to start the new day. "Lead off, amigo!" he said to Alvar.

As they entered the lower pasture that held the heavies, Alvar instructed J.W. to ride slow and easy among the cows looking for any that might be in distress and needing help. "But how am I gonna know that?"

"Oh, you will know senor, you will know. When you see one, wave your hat or whistle so I can come and help. Most

72

B. N. Rundell

will do just fine on their own, if you look out yonder you'll see several new calves already, but some will have a hard time. Sit easy and watch, Oh, and watch for coyotes, they are bad and should be keeled before they get the calves."

"O.K. then, let's do it, I spose."

Walking slow and easy through the scattered herd, J.W. searched for any cows with any signs of distress. There was a big red momma cow that was licking the afterbirth off a brand new baby, two others that apparently had their calves in the night but J.W. didn't see any others that were doing anything but grazing or laying down and contentedly chewing their cud with a far off look in their eyes that said, 'Don't bother me.' With several looks over his shoulder toward the main house in anticipation of seeing Florence coming to join them, J.W. stopped his mount, curled his left leg over the pommel and leaned on the saddle horn to casually survey the nearby cows for any that might be out of sorts. Although social animals, cows are more solitary than horses and usually preferred their own space. He noticed one heavy working her way slowly to the edge of the herd and appeared to be seeking a spot of her own for some privacy. He watched her carefully and waited. The solitary cow, mostly black with a splash of white across her face, slowly walked around in a semblance of a circle, stopped, dropped her head just a mite, and seemed to be grunting or pushing. With her tail raised, J.W. was mesmerized as he watched the beginnings of the birth, the cow slowly pushed. First J.W. noticed what appeared to be a small white hoof, *no, there's two hooves* he thought. Then came a shiny, wet black nose and moment by moment and ever so slowly came the rest of the head, a pause by the cow to breathe deeply, then the rest of the front legs and the shoulders, another pause and very quickly the rest of the calf seemed to squirt into the world and drop behind the momma. The black cow turned, sniffed, examined and began licking the calf to stir it to breathe and move. J.W. was not disappointed and sat erect and smiled thinking, *Now ain't that sumpin'.* But without realizing it, he

73

spoke aloud and was answered by a voice from behind him, "Yes, it's something alright. I never get tired of watching that," said Flo as she spurred the palomino alongside Smoke. She stood in her stirrups and looked over the cattle, dropped into the saddle and said, "Looks like we've got a few new babies out there," and turning to J.W. asked, "So, how's the mid-wife doing?"

J.W. looked at Flo and grinned, then with a chuckle replied, "All right, I reckon, ain't even had to get off my horse and that suits me just fine."

"Well, don't get too complacent, there will be some days like that but others that keep you on the ground and pulling calves one after another and you'll get so wet and slick with their goo that you'll think you're the newborn calf and you'll be wantin' some ol' cow to come and lick you clean and dry." She giggled as she held that image in her mind. "Boy, I'd like to see that!" and giggled again with a hand to her mouth and smiling at J.W.

"Fuuunnny, maybe you'd look just as funny rollin' around in the mess like a baby calf!"

Both J.W. and Florence were laughing when Flo noticed something out of the corner of her eye that sobered her. Standing in her stirrups, she looked at the far edge of the herd and saw a cow lumbering away with belly bouncing and something chasing. Flo dropped to her seat and as she spurred Blondie she hollered at J.W. "Come on!" Without hesitation he spurred Smoke and set out after the palomino with his girl laying along her neck and digging her heels into its side. As they neared the fleeing cow, J.W. saw the pursuer was a coyote that was repeatedly jumping at the hind end of the cow. He saw the cow had started birthing and the calf was partially hanging out, front feet and head exposed and the coyote was trying to get at the calf. An angry Flo pointed and yelled at J.W. "Shoot it! Shoot it!"

J.W. dug his spurs into the grey, felt a surge from the horse and drew his Navy Colt. Pulling alongside the bouncing bloody scene, he fired, missed, fired again and the coyote tumbled end over end. He sat deep in his saddle, pulled on the reins and returned to the coyote that was on its side but trying to rise. He shot it again, this time in the head, to ensure the end of the predator. Reining around to see where Flo was, he saw the palomino standing near the cow, and Flo was beside the cow with one hand resting on its back. J.W. pulled his horse down to a walk, dropped off and ground tied it, then walked slowly to the side of Florence. She instructed, "Stand near her head, I'm gonna see if I can save the calf."

J.W. walked to the side of the cow's neck, dropped a hand to touch her and spoke softly to give reassurance. Flo went to the back of the cow and looked at the calf. She mumbled an "Oh no, that's what I was afraid of," and reached for the hooves. She spoke to J.W., "I'm gonna try to help by pulling, try to keep her as still as you can." Flo grabbed the hooves, put one foot on the hind end and pulled. That was all the cow needed and with a big push from the cow, the calf came forth and dropped to the ground. Flo moved away and let the mother cow turn and examine her calf. Stepping back to the side of J.W. she said, "That calf's not gonna make it. The coyote took its tongue. I tell you, if I had my way, I'd kill every coyote on the face of this earth! I hate 'em! That's so unfair, that calf didn't have a chance!" She turned and buried her face in the chest of J.W. and sobbed as she beat on his chest. J.W. put one arm around her and held her close without saying a word, and waited for her tantrum to subside. He understood her emotions but reveled in the intimate moment.

She stopped beating on his chest, sniffled and turned her face to rest her cheek against him. Reaching into her pocket, she pulled out a small hanky and dabbed her tears, blew her nose and without looking up at J.W. said, "You must think I'm some kind of baby, cryin' over a calf!"

"No, I think you're pretty wonderful."

She turned her face upward to look at this man that held her and he bent to kiss her expectant lips. It was a simple and

short kiss but she smiled at him and said, "I was wonderin'
when you'd do that," and flashed another smile at him.

"That's the first time I ever kissed a girl," he stated.

Again she looked up at him as he relaxed his arm that held
her and she smiled with a "Good, let's just keep it that way. I
don't want you to ever kiss any other girl."

His embarrassed smile down at her upturned face gave her
the answer she sought and she dropped her face to his chest
again as he drew her tight against him with his strong arms.

"Are you two sweethearts going to stand there like that all
day or are we going to geet some work done?" shouted a
smiling vaquero.

The two quickly stepped back from one another and J.W.
waved at the vaquero as he rode up to the pair. "I see you got
the coyote that did thees. Good shooting, but now you need to
drag that calf over to the draw yonder and cover eet with some
rocks so no more coyotes will come around."

J.W. nodded his agreement and set about the assigned task.
The rest of the day passed without any unusual incident, two
more births without any need of help and one still birth that
had to be disposed. J.W. and Florence stayed near one another
and their broad smiles resulted in both of them catching more
than their share of dust in their teeth, but they couldn't help
themselves. They were simply following the age old practice
of young people falling in love. But the day drew to an end and
they returned to the headquarters, put up the horses and went
their separate ways, Florence to the main house and J.W. to the
bunk house. But both were thinking about a walk together after
supper.

Chapter Fourteen

Trouble

HOPPY MADE A PRACTICE of rotating the duties among the men to keep the variety and interest high. He knew a worker that was bored with routine was a man that would become careless in his duties, but one that stayed attentive and interested would also learn other skills and be an overall better hand. This morning's assignment of mid-wife for the heavies fell to Jake and Skinny, Monty and Sean would work the North East pasture, Patrick and Shamus would oversee the South East hills and J.W. and Alvar were assigned the West pasture and thickets. As the men walked to the corral, Jake sidled along J.W. and chuckled as he asked, "Hey, the way you talked after the brother's fixed you with that raised bunk, everbody thot you'd get back at 'em and ain't nuthin' happened. Did you chicken out, or just decide to leave sleepin' dogs lie?" J.W. knew Jake was often buddying up with Patrick and J.W. thought he was just trying to find out if anything was planned that he could take back to Patrick. J.W. answered Jake with, "Oh, I dunno, I guess I just been too busy to think much about it," without giving Jake any tale to tell.

"Ah, you ain't gonna do nuthin' cuz you know Patrick'll clean yore plow," chuckled Jake as he walked away with his chaps flopping loosely around his legs. J.W. just smiled at the retreating cowboy and knew that by waiting to seek his pay back, the recipient would become less guarded and more easily pranked. Following Alvar to the corral for their horses, J. W. laughed quietly to himself as he pictured his planned prank and the response it would garner.

The Western part of the ranch held a wide stretch of grazing land with several kinds of grasses and graze. Scattered thickets, usually at the mouth of a ravine from the hills, were made up of Sassafras, Burr Oak and scrub oak brush. Along the low dry hills, Juniper dotted the slopes with scattered patches of a variety of cactus and rock outcroppings. Most cattle would stay in the green grass as long as water was plentiful, but there were always those ol' mossy horns that preferred the protection of the hills and the dryer graze. J.W. lost the coin flip and was directed by Alvar to ride the hills and kick out any cows to the flats. As J.W. moved Smoke up the clay of the hillside, he spoke to his faithful companion with, "Well, Smoke ol' boy. This is more like it, I was gettin' tired of all that belly deep grass and those wet swales and not bein' able to see very far with them rollin' hills. Weren't you? I like it better up here just far enough above everything to see farther and know what's around ya." He reached down and patted the neck of the steel dust, rose back up and started whistling a random tune.

A couple of hours and a few miles later, J.W. spotted a brindle big horned steer trying to hide behind the largest Juniper on the hillside. Acting like he hadn't seen the steer, J.W. used knee pressure to turn his mount to pass by the tree on the uphill side. Keeping his eyes averted, J.W. continued his whistling and when he reached his preferred point uphill from the steer, he suddenly turned Smoke and spurred to charge the rogue animal. His tactic worked, the startled steer leaped, bellowed and took off straight downhill to escape the mounted threat. Zigzagging through the trees and mesquite, J.W. kept up the chase, sometimes almost bumping into the steer, until they hit the flats and the beast quickened his pace thinking only distance would save him. He was right as J.W. reined up and waved his hat at the fleeing brindle. Wiping his sweaty forehead with his shirt sleeve, he turned back to the Juniper and some shade to take his nooning.

The rest of the day was a copy of the morning with two other cows found on the hillsides and successfully driven to the flats. J.W. had been watchful for a necessary prop for his planned prank and had almost given up finding what he sought, but just before deciding to return to the designated meeting point with Alvar, he spotted what he had been looking for. A cluster of boulders just downhill from a couple of big Junipers had a flat sunny spot on a big granite stone that held just what he wanted. The shed skin of a rattlesnake that was intact and almost four feet long beckoned the man. He laughed as he thought about Patrick's response, it was no secret that the man held a hatred and fear of snakes and rattlesnakes were the worst. Using a couple of saved strings from tobacco pouches, he tied off one end of the skin and slowly filled the skin with sandy soil and tied off the other end. He hoisted the snakeskin with both hands, smiled and turned to drop it into his saddle bags. Mounting up he kneed Smoke toward the meeting place.

Tired cowboys littered the grounds around headquarters with some by the corral, either seated and leaning against the fence with others standing with one foot on the bottom rail. Others were leaning back in ladder back chairs near the bunkhouse door. J.W. and Monty were stretched out on their bunks. Two stragglers walked slowly from the barn but Skinny leaned against the side of the Cook shack waiting for the bell. When Cooky stepped out holding the triangle and striker, Skinny was the first in line and the clanging alarm brought the rest of the hungry men. Monty strode quickly to the door of the bunkhouse and asked J.W., "Ya comin'?"

J.W. answered, "Sure I am, just gotta get my boots on!"

When he was alone, J.W. quickly withdrew the snakeskin from his saddlebags, walked swiftly to Patrick's bunk and slipped it under the covers. He knew it would not be noticed in the rumpled bed, but he arranged the covers just enough to ensure his plan would work. He trotted to his bunk, quickly put on his boots and still beat a couple of the slower workers to the cook shack.

Maintaining his routine, after supper J.W. strolled the grounds practicing his roping trying once again to catch that pesky rabbit that teased him every night. Soon joined by Florence, she put her hand through the crook of his left arm and they walked and talked. Since it was nearing the end of the week, their conversation turned to their work with the Sunday School and the progress of the different students. As dusk began to drop darkness across the flats, the couple had timed their walk to reach the side of the far tack shed when visibility was absent. J.W. stole a couple of willingly surrendered kisses and after a long embrace, they stepped from behind the shed and continued their walk to the house. After Florence turned on the porch and threw him a kiss, he returned to the bunkhouse. Dark thirty brought all the residents of the bunk house inside and most prepared to climb into their bunks. J.W. had his back to the rest of the occupants but continued his routine of shucking his boots, britches and hat before leaning back and pulling up the covers. A casual glance revealed Patrick and his brothers also getting ready to climb in their bunks. J.W. rolled to his side with his back to the rest of the crew, chuckling to himself.

Seconds later the bunkhouse erupted with a loud scream and the ruffling of blankets as Patrick jumped to the foot of the bed and stood back pointing and yelling, "Snake! Snake! There's a huge snake in my bunk! Get it, somebody! Get that thing!" He was prancing and hopping from barefoot to barefoot. The rest of the men started laughing and looked to J.W. still lying with his back to the men but unable to keep from shaking as he laughed.

"Shamus! Get a stick or sumpin' and get that snake outta there!" screamed Patrick as he ordered his brother to action. Shamus ran from the bunkhouse to the barn, retrieved a pitchfork and returned, with Patrick yelling and screaming all the while. The men continued laughing but no one dared move the covers just in case it was a real live snake. No one liked snakes and any cowboy knows the dangers of a rattlesnake, be it diamond back, messasauga, or timber rattlesnake. Many a time a rattlesnake had spooked a horse that in turn dumped a cowboy on the rocks, and all ranch hands despised the rattlers. As Patrick stood and pointed, Shamus pulled the covers back with the tines of the pitchfork very slowly. When he first saw the realistic looking snakeskin, he jumped and dropped the covers. Patrick screamed and jumped back as the bunkhouse erupted in laughter again. Comments were heard like, "Sounds like a girl, don't he?" and "Glad it weren't my bunk."

Slowly Shamus tried again, lifted the covers and pulled them back so as not to startle the snake. All the men drew quiet as they could see the skin and thought sure it was a live one and a big one. Shamus continued and finally revealed the whole snake and the bunkhouse sighed in relief. The anger welled up in Patrick as he demanded Shamus, "Get rid of that thing!" and continuing said, "Whoever did this is goin' ta' get it!" then realizing it was probably the vengeance of J.W., he yelled, "Greenhorn! Greenhorn!" without response from J.W. "Harpold! Harpold!" and J.W. slowly rolled over to face Patrick.

"What are you yellin' about Patrick? Can't a man get any sleep?"

"You know what I'm yellin' about!" he yelled as he stomped the length of the bunkhouse to face the man he saw as an intruder. J.W. stood, having quickly stomped into his boots, as Patrick approached. Patrick started to poke J.W. in the chest to intimidate him as he was yelling, "You did that! You put the snake in my bunk!" But J.W. quickly grabbed his finger and bent it back and quietly warned, "Don't go pokin' at me."

Patrick scowled as J.W. continued to bend his finger. When he let go, the oldest McPherson tried to stand tall as he had so often to intimidate the usually smaller men he picked on, but tall as he was, he was still eye to eye with J.W. Squinting his eyes he snarled, "I should stomp you into the ground, right now!"

"Won't work," responded J.W.

"Whatdya mean, it won't work? I can stomp you anytime,"

"Not now you can't."

"Why not?" whined the bully.

"Cuz you'd need to pack a lunch to last long enough and the cook shack's closed. Ya better wait till tomorrow," chuckled J.W. turning slightly away from his antagonist.

Patrick grabbed J.W.'s shoulder to spin him back and as he did, Patrick threw a right fist at his jaw. J.W. leaned back just enough the let the fist fly by but he grabbed Patrick's arm with both hands, brought it down as he raised his knee and smashed it with a sold thud. J.W. slacked a bit not wanting to break Patrick's arm, just make it plenty sore.

Patrick started a back swing trying to elbow the face of J.W. and once again missed. J.W. brought his swing from the floor right into the wind of his attacker doubling him over. Clasping his hands together, J.W. brought them down on the back of the neck of Patrick, dropping him on his face to the floor. He didn't try to rise for several moments, then putting his hands beside his chest, he slowly rose to a seating position, glared at J.W. and snarled, "This ain't over."

"You might want to rethink that. As far as I'm concerned, it is over. Let it lie."

Still grumbling, Patrick returned to his bunk, but drew back the covers to make sure there were no more surprises. The rest of the men had quietly returned to their bunks knowing that when the owner's oldest son was riled, it was always best to keep your distance. The last candle was extinguished but it was some time before the usual chorus of snores filled the bunk house.

Chapter Fifteen

Roping

THE VAQUERO AND HIS PARTNER, J.W. were back in the Western pasture and the nearby hills when the grey sky of early morn told of the breaking of the new day. Their responsibility was to find any hide-out heavies, count the unbranded cattle and calves, and check for any sign of Comanche or other Indians prowling around the cattle. Alvar told J.W. this would be a good time to put his practice to work and do some roping. "Today you weel learn to rope da' heels of the cow and stretch heem out so sheee don' fight no more."

Alvar demonstrated the size of loop to build and how to throw it so it would lay up against the hind legs to let the animal step into it, pull the slack and dally. "When we cut out a cow, you weeel rope its horns and I'll show you how to heel." He instructed J.W. to work around the small herd and pick out the red brindle near the edge. "When you rope her, dally queeeck and pull her away, I'll come up behind and drop the heel loop," directed Alvar.

J.W. spotted the brindle Alvar pointed out and worked his way toward the cow. Building his loop, he held his hand down beside his leg with the edge of the loop tucked under his arm. Nearing the cow, the brindle looked back at the approaching cowboy, perceived no threat and dropped her head to graze. As the horse drew nearer, the cow snatched up her head in alarm and turned to run but J.W., after one swing of the loop over his head stretched out the rope and the loop dropped over the cow's horns to instantly be pulled tight from both the jerking of the slack by J.W. and the beginning flight of the cow. A quick dally and the cow hit the end of the rope but J.W. had already reined his horse to pull to the side and the taut rope jerked the cow around and with his spurs into the steel dust ribs, his horse dragged the cow away from the herd. Alvar was quick to the rear of the cow and with one swing of his riata he dropped the loop to momentarily stand on its edge in front of the rear legs of the cow. Unknowingly stepping into the loop and with Alvar instantly pulling slack, a quick dally around the big horn of the Mex saddle and the reining away of the gelding, the cow was stretched out between the riders.

"See, just like that! Now throw your slack so the loop will drop and we'll try it again," instructed the vaquero. The cow quickly stepped free of the heel loop but fought against the loop around her horns as she tossed her head trying to free herself from the entanglement. J.W. rode closer to give more slack to let the riata's loop enlarge and it soon fell free.

"Now, let's just practice a leetle wit' the heel loop. Just walk up behind a cow and try throwing your loop like theees," he said as he demonstrated on a nearby cow. Without Alvar pulling the slack the cow deftly stepped across the loop and continued with minimal aggravation. J.W. followed suit and laid a loop in front of the hind legs of a nearby cow, let it lay and again the cow stepped on through.

The men continued with their survey of the cattle and the checking of the breaks and thickets for any hide outs, but with every approach, J.W. would through a loop to the hind legs, and let the cow pass through. After their noon break at the mouth of a brush filled ravine and under the shade of a pair of sassafras trees, Alvar told his protégé they would try to put his practice to work at the first opportunity.

They rode together in a zig-zag pattern, first checking the cattle in the pasture, back to the hills and ravines, and back to the pasture. The direction of their ride was dictated by the location of cattle. As they rode the up and down of the hills and ravines, J.W. spotted another old mossy horn trying to hide out among the junipers and scrub oak and with a whistle and a wave to Alvar, they put their plan into action. Alvar worked from the side of the juniper, jumped the big cow and dropped a loop over her head. With his dally secure he started to pull the stubborn cow down the slight hill and J.W. started his pursuit and within moments he was in position to throw his heel loop.

He deftly laid it in front of the rear hooves, but the smart old cow drug her hooves and collapsed the loop. Quickly coiling in his riata, J.W. built another loop all the while in close pursuit through the junipers and brush, finally he was able to again throw his heel loop and this time he was able to snatch his slack and discovered he had successfully caught one hind hoof. Now the cow was mad and fought by kicking at the heel loop and tossing her head in protest at the rope on her horns. The cow succeeded freeing her hind leg and lowering her head started after the big black Andalusia and the wide-eyed vaquero.

With blood in her eyes, the mad cow gained ground on the Andalusia and the vaquero sought escape from the clay hills and scattered junipers. He knew if he could get in the clear, he could drag the cow off her feet and protect his horse. The dust and dirt were flying and branches of juniper were stretching out to lash the face and legs of the vaquero but within moments he gained the flats with the cow now dropping her heels and trying to overpower her captor.

J.W. was right behind them and had a loop built and ready but when Alvar hit the clear he immediately reined to the side and let the strength of the big black jerk the cow off balance.

With a thud, a bellow and a cloud of dust, the cow hit the dirt and hooked one horn in the ground twisting her neck. The momentum flipped the cow end for end and she landed with heels toward Alvar and head toward J.W. The mossy horn jumped to her feet and started to charge toward J.W., hit the end of the rope and switched ends but her rage fueled another charge and once again she was after the black. Alvar spurred his mount to escape and the charge of the cow brought her horns to the side of the horse but the sharp tips hit just behind Alvar's leg into the fender of the saddle and the lower horn went into the tapadero with Alvar's boot. The impact moved the Andalusia but motivated him as well and his resulting jump freed the horns and took the vaquero out of reach of the cow.

Suddenly the cow was stretched out as J.W. successfully heeled the beast and pulled her back. With the cow stretched between them, horses and men drew breath and smiled at one another. Alvar shouted, "Let me throw slack first, we'll let our ropes drop and follow her to get them. No more fighting!" J.W. nodded in agreement and as soon as Alvar threw slack, J.W. pulled the cow off balance and she fell, giving J.W. a chance to drop his riata and escape up the hill far enough to discourage any pursuit from the angered cow. The old mossy horn bellowed her belligerence as she ran toward the pasture throwing her head to free her horns from the nuisance. Within less than two hundred feet, both riatas were in the dirt and the two men were picking them up.

"Whoooeee, that cow, she was maaaad," declared Alvar, stating the obvious.

"For a minute there, I thought she was going to run you through with them horns."

At the reminder, Alvar looked down at the fender beneath his leg and noticed the puncture hole, lifted the leather to see if his horse had been injured and showed a smile of relief as he saw no damage. Pointing at the puncture, he said, "That hole will be a reminder for me to be more careful next time. If he hit my leg, that would have been mucho painful."

Both men laughed together as they dropped their coiled riatas over their saddle horns and continued their survey. The remainder of the afternoon passed without incident, even though the partners practiced on a couple more cows. With the sun low in the West, Alvar was riding along the edge of the ridges and draws while J.W. was higher up and weaving through the junipers. Of a sudden, Alvar's attention was drawn to the far slope of a slight hill as J.W. whooped and shouted, "Here we come, get ready!" Amidst a cloud of dust, J.W. spurred Smoke towards the startled vaquero and dragging behind him was a protesting buck white tail deer that was fighting the rope around his horns. With a broad smile and a shouted "EEEEeehahhh!" Alvar gave pursuit, knowing he was expected to heel the prancing deer. It was all J.W. could do to stay ahead of the fleet buck and it was only because the taut rope jerked the deer back and forth as he fought. With the Andalusia enthusiastically entering the race, the vaquero was soon in position to drop a heel loop, but the prancing and jumping of the deer wasn't the same as the expected stepping into a loop by a cow, and it took several attempts until the vaquero finally timed his throw to capture both hind legs of the buck. With his usual quick dally and turn, the vaquero stretched out the buck amidst the laughter and hoots of the two men.

"You are crazy senor! No one ropes a deer but a crazy cowboy!"

J.W. laughed and as both men nodded, they threw the slack to release the buck. Without hesitation the nearly exhausted and bewildered animal bounded away dragging J.W.'s riata with him. "Now you'll have to chase after heem to get your riata, senor. Serves you right, you crazy . . . " and finished his remark with a long laugh. J.W. pointed his grey after the buck and trotted off to retrieve his riata.

As the two partners entered the grounds of the headquarters, they were laughing again as they recalled their adventures of the day. Observed by Patrick and Shamus, Patrick growled to his brother, "I'm gonna get that greenhorn, he's gonna pay for what he did."

"But Pa told you to drop it, Patrick, we got him with the bunk and now he did his snake thing, so Pa said drop it."

"Maybe so, but I'm still gonna get him," then looking at his brother added, ". . .sides, he ain't done nothin' to you and Sean and you two were just as much a part of it. You two better watch out cuz I'm thinkin' he's gonna try to do somethin' on you two."

Shamus looked at Patrick and considered what he said then mumbled, "Maybe you're right. I better say sumpin' to Sean. We don't wanna get caught like you did."

Patrick grumbled as the two brothers walked toward the main house. This was Saturday and the family ate supper together on Saturdays. As they walked up the steps, Patrick added, "And he's been chousin' around Flo too much. I'm thinkin' she needs to stay away from him. He ain't good enough for her, and I sure don't want him marryin' up with her and makin' him part of the family. That just ain't right."

Chapter Sixteen

Kids

THE THREE BROTHERS and J.W. were joined by Monty as they trailed the buckboard into the village for the Sunday activities. J.W. moved closer behind the buckboard to visit with Flo as she rode the makeshift quilt covered seat facing to the rear. The occasional over the shoulder glances from her mother reassured Florence of her mother's listening ear to the conversations. The couple confined their discussion to the plans for the Sunday School and the different students. With summer well under way, the usual dusty road was excelling itself with the powdery dust that settled on all the trailing cowboys and J.W. was forced to join them as they dropped further back from the buckboard. Siding up with the older Monty, the two began sharing common experiences of the green forests of the Midwest.

"Yeah, back when I was a younker, I used to spend all day in the woods goin' after them red tailed squirrels with my slingshot. I'd usually get at least one or two fer Ma to make a good stew with. Them woods was full of them thangs. Then ever onct in a while, I'd bring home some turtles fer a little variety," shared the slightly graying man that sat easy in his saddle. Monty exuded a cautious confidence and was respected by the others as a man to ride the river with.

"I had an old mountain man I used to follow around and he would teach me things about the different animals and such. I had an old New Bedford flintlock, thirty-six caliber, that I'd take out and shoot whatever'd fit in the pot. Then sometimes I'd take my cane pole and go after some bluegill, catch a mess and Ma'd fry 'em up. Boy Howdy, them was some good eatin'. Ma'd tell me to be careful as I was eatin' 'em, she'd say, 'Boy, yore gonna knock yourself out, why yore tongue's flappin' so hard yore gonna beatchur brains in wid it.' Then she'd smile at me and pass the plate with more filets," recalled J.W. with a wistful look chasing away the smile.

Monty smiled and dropped his head so no one could see the tear of remembrance that threatened to cut loose from his eye. Men that have been long separated from hearth and home can be as wistful as a heart broken old maid when they let their minds chase memories. Monty would never share what brought the tear nor admit he ever had the tear, but his glassy eyed stare shut out the world and told of pictures of the past, both fond and sad. The rest of the ride to town was heralded with silence as the thoughts brought about by the brief recollection caused everyone to dabble in the distant past and recall friends and adventures long tucked away.

The morning service followed the familiar format with the pastor leading the singing and bringing the message. This morning's thoughts were centered on James 4:14 *Whereas ye know not what shall be on the morrow. For what is your life? It is even a vapor, that appeareth for a little time, and then vanisheth away.* He asked those present to consider their lives and for what purpose they were on this earth. But by the time the pastor asked the question, most were already thinking about the good food that was waiting.

J.W. and Florence took their familiar seat on the tail end of the buck board and were talking about their lessons planned for the afternoon's school when Patrick strode up to them scowling at J.W. and said, "I thought I told you to stay away from my sister!"

Florence jumped down from her seat and grabbed her brother's arm so he would look at her and said, "Patrick McPherson, you know very well that Pa told you to leave us alone, and 'us' means both me and J.W.!" she yelled up at her big brother. Patrick grinned and looked back at J.W. and said, "So now you're hidin' behind her skirts, I see."

"I ain't hidin' nowhere, but this ain't the time or the place," responded J.W. leaning into his words.

Patrick stuttered and looked around for something to take out his anger and slapped J.W.'s cup of lemonade off the tailgate, snarled back at J.W. and turned and stomped off. Florence stood with hands on her hips and stomped her feet saying, "That Patrick makes me so mad, I'd like to kick him!"

"I coulda done that for you if'n I thought that's really what you wanted," replied J.W. with a sober expression.

Florence looked at him and ducked her head, giggled a moment and turned and hopped back on the tailgate of the buckboard seating herself a bit closer to J.W. The young man reached around behind her, put his hand on her waist and pulled her even closer to the accompanying giggles of the happy girl.

School had settled into a familiar routine with the same seven students faithfully attending. Occasionally a cowboy or two or a parent would sit in on the classes, but the class was stable at seven. Grace and Elizabeth, both seven, were progressing nicely in McGuffey's first reader while the Rundle twins, Dan and Don, were bickering over the Primer. Florence had Don start reading the review of lesson five and he began, *"The cat and the rat ran. Ann sat, and Nat ran."* Florence then had the boys switch off with Dan taking the thin book and starting, *"a rat ran at Nat. Can Ann fan the lad?"* "Where'd the rat go?" asked Dan as Don snickered. Dan without looking, back-handed his brother across the jaw. "Boys, boys! Enough of that, now apologize to your brother!" instructed Flo. Both boys looked at each other, ducked their heads and mumbled, "Sorry." Florence was exasperated because she only thought Dan should apologize because he hit Don, but now she didn't know which one was which and with a breath of exasperation started to instruct again when she was interrupted by Don asking, "And what happened to Nat? Did he get hot or sumpin' so's Ann would fan him?" Ignoring his question, Florence said, "Let's just go on. Now boys, I want you to share the book and study the words and pictures on the next page. It begins with a picture of an ax and the name beside it. See there?" she asked as she pointed at the page. "Now you two work on that page and the words while I give Grace and Elizabeth their lesson.

The girls perked up and scooted to the edge of the bench as Florence sat on a ladder-back chair in front of them holding McGuffey's First reader. Pointing with the end of the quill pen, she said, "Now girls, I want you to read together as I point with the quill at the words."

Both girls smiled broadly and began to read together, "*Ned is on the box. He has a pen in his hand. A big rat is in the box.*" At the mention of the rat, both girls wrinkled their nose at the thought and giggled at one another.

While Florence continued to work with her four students, J.W. was directing his students giving them assignments to work on while he worked with them individually. Since the two girls had to share the Third Reader, J.W. chose to keep them on the same assignment and lesson seventy-nine was the poem *Good Night.* He had the girls reading to each other and taking turns with each paragraph. Gabriella began, "*The sun is hidden from our sight, the birds are sleeping sound . . .*" she continued until the end of the paragraph and Olivia commenced with "*Good night, my father, mother, dear! Now kiss your little son:*" at the mention of 'son', Olivia said, "I'm not a son, I'm a daughter. I'm going to change it!" But J.W. had to step in to the tantrum and added, "O.K. if you want to change it to 'daughter' then you have to find a word that rhymes with 'daughter' or you can't finish your reading!" Wrinkling her brow, she thought, mouthed some words, thought some more and frustrated at her failure said, "Oh, alright, I'll leave it like that," and continued to read picking up with, *"Good night, my friends, both far and near! Good night to everyone."*

With the girls returning to their assignment, J.W. focused on the older boy, Josiah. The older boy was struggling but making good progress but it was necessary to have him in only the Second Reader, which, because of his embarrassment, he kept obscured from the other's sight. Sensitive to his concerns, J.W. worked quietly with him so the others wouldn't hear the level of the lesson assigned to Josiah. He had the boy working with lesson seventy-one, the reading of a lullaby. He began, *"Sweet and low, sweet and low, Wind of the western sea, . . ."* and looking up at J.W. said, "I like the way that sounds and the way it reads," with a smile spreading across his face. J.W. put his hand on the boy's shoulder and gave an encouraging squeeze.

When the kids scattered to the winds and the 'teachers' finished the re-arranging of benches and other duties, J.W. stepped to the side of the door to let Florence walk before him. After Florence's pleading with her mother to intervene on her behalf and keep 'father and the boys' at home, the couple was looking forward to their ride home without any other chaperones. There was nothing improper on their minds, but to have the uninterrupted and unaccompanied two hours together was something they treasured. The casual and comfortable ride to the ranch gave opportunity to talk about a possible future together. Florence considered their being together forever a sure thing but as she chattered about their own home and children, J.W. still held apprehensive thoughts tight. Not that he didn't want a future with Flo, he did, but he wasn't sure it could not happen with her Pa and brothers so dead set against it. He realized she had asked him a question and he said, "What, I didn't hear you," as he looked at her inquiringly.

"You just weren't paying attention! I said, how many children do you want?" she asked again with a coy bowed head feigning embarrassment.

"Uh, I guess I never thought much about it. I would like a son though, and a daughter too I guess, maybe more."

"I want at least four! Two boys and two girls!" declared Flo with a giggle, and added, "Maybe more."

"And just how am I goin' to make enough money to feed all you hungry females?" kidded J.W.

"Oh, you'll work it out. I've got confidence in you. You'll make a great dad!"

The tidbits of tantalizing dreams and hopes accompanied them all the way back to the ranch. As they rode through the towering gate at the adobe wall, the shadows of the long past dusk had been replaced with dark corners and scattered shafts of lamp light. Riding up to the hitch rail at the edge of the veranda, a voice boomed from the darkness, "Out a little late with me daughter, I see. I'll not be havin' that, ye hear me?" and as his anger boiled he added firmly, "Ye see me boy, when a man and a woman are out in the dark alone, people talk. A man can live it down, but a girl cannot. Ye'll not be doing that again!" he stated with finality.

As Florence clambered down from her saddle, she started to plead with her father, but was firmly pushed toward the door and admonished, "Hush girl, this is man's work!"

J.W. remained mounted, bent down to take the reins of the palomino, and as he started to turn away, answered, "Yessir, Mr. McPherson, you are right. It will not happen again. There is nothing more important to me than Flo and I'll not want to do anything that would cause her any embarrassment or trouble. Yessir." His response stymied the angry Scotsman who stood stuttering and raised a fist to the back of the departing cowboy. Stomping his foot, he turned and followed his daughter into the house.

The palomino had a separate stall in the barn and was always kept away from the ranch horses, so J.W. dismounted by the corral and looped Smoke's rein over the second rail, and led the palomino into the barn to strip the gear. Within moments he had rubbed down the mare, fed her some oats and as he was shutting the stall door, he had a thought. The ranch milk cow was kept in a larger stall at the end of the barn and J.W. grabbed the lamp from the post, walked to the cow's stall and looked around. Spotting what he wanted, he looked around for a container and seeing an old empty can used to scoop oats, grabbed it and retrieved his prize. As he was exiting the barn, he sat the can down by the edge of the door and walked to the corral to tend to his gelding.

With darkness well upon them, J.W. eased into the bunkhouse so as not to awaken any that might have turned in early, but there were several lamps and candles burning as the men had gathered toward the rear of the bunkhouse and were shooting dice. The continual chatter and outbursts of laughter caught his attention and he casually strolled to see what was happening. As he neared, Skinny called out, "There he is, the Romeo of the Ranch! Howdy, J.W.!" The brothers turned to look at the approaching man and Patrick scowled, muttered, "Oh, it's him. Come on, who's shootin'?" he asked about the next turn at the dice.

Speaking a little lower, Skinny asked, "Ya wanna join us?"

"Nah, I'm beat, I think I'll turn in," he said with a big yawn and a shrug of his shoulders as he turned away. A muttered, "We didn't want him anyway," from Patrick was ignored and J.W. walked back to his bunk. He shucked his clothes and crawled under the covers, rolled to his side facing away from the crew, and chuckled to himself. He knew he would sleep light and would make his move in the wee hours of the morning.

When his eyes opened to the darkness, J.W. lay still and listened. The bunkhouse was filled with snores and snorts with an occasional murmured phrase from a restless sleeper. J.W. casually slipped from his bunk and headed to the door acting like he was anxious to get to the privy. And he did go to the privy, but on the way back he detoured to the barn. With enough moonlight to keep from stubbing his toes, J.W. made it back to the bunkhouse and quietly entered. He waited by the door for his eyes to become accustomed to the dark interior. Then he stealthily moved to the side of Shamus' bunk, did his deed and went back to the door. Stepping outside, he tossed the can on a pile of hay by the corral and re-entered the bunkhouse. He carefully and quietly got back into his bunk and covered up. Two bunks away, Monty grinned and rolled over to await the action.

Chapter Seventeen

Roundup

WITH OPEN RANGE and neighboring ranches using some common areas, most ranchers found it necessary to keep up on the branding. When the new calf crop is on the ground and weaned or close to weaning, the round-up of pairs was necessary. With larger herds it was always probable that some would be missed and it was common to find some mavericks with the herd and those could be last year's calves or even from previous years. Often ranchers would build a complex of corrals farther out into a central area of the graze for the purpose of branding while others would just work the herd into an area of flat and graze and work strictly with ropes. The McPherson ranch shunned corrals and fences except for those within the grounds at headquarters but those were mainly for horses and breaking new mounts. This week would be spent entirely on the round-up, sorting and branding for the new calves and mavericks. It was shaping up to be a busy one.

Hoppy had kept the same men in the usual pastures for the last ten days and today would be done likewise, except all the cattle were to be brought to the low meadow just below headquarters. In anticipation of the long days, Hoppy slammed the door of the bunkhouse open with his left hand and thrust in a lamp with his right. He hollered at the men, "We're burnin' daylight! Roll out and git a move on, we got round-up and brandin' to get done. Cooky's already waitin' fer ya so git a move on!" He stomped out the door as a couple of lamps were turned up to give the men enough light to find their britches and boots. J.W. was quickly dressed and as he approached the door, he heard a loud, "EEeeeooooooo! What th'...!" As J.W. disappeared out the door, other men looked at Shamus and asked, "What's the matter with you?"

The men watched as Shamus crossed his legs and cupped the heel of his boot in his hand, felt something and dropped his foot to the floor, stood up and placed the toe of one boot against the heel of the other and tugged to free his foot. All the while he had a snarl on his face that wrinkled his nose and all the way across his forehead. He finally freed his foot but fell back on his bunk with his stockinged feet up in the air and everyone said, "Eeeeewwwh," as they saw the sock that had been dipped in the fresh cowpie in the bottom of his boot. Shamus screamed, "I'm gonna kill him!" as the men let loose with a bunkhouse rocking round of laughter. They all noticed the absence of J.W. and knew he was already at the cook shack. J.W. did fill up a plate at the cook shack, but he retreated to the back side of the barn before the rest of the men made their appearance at the breakfast table.

Alvar caught up with J.W. a little later as they headed for the West pasture and the duties for the day. It promised to be a long day for the pair as their assigned area was larger and rougher than the others, but both men enjoyed the varied terrain more than the continual rolling grasslands of the other pastures. Overall the ranch encompassed about 140,000 acres, but the open range was hard to calculate ownership as there was none. The West pasture and hills covered about 80,000 of those acres but J.W. often thought if there was a way to flatten it out, it would be twice as large.

The team worked well together, they would switch off heading and heeling as the situation required, but most often they would just drive the animals in the designated direction. To get them out of the hills and ravines, the men would work together with one riding the ridges and the other clearing the draws. The one in the draws had the more difficult part with the need to work through the thick brush and kick out any stragglers. All the men had been instructed to take their bedrolls and enough supplies for three days. Camping out in the pastures or hills would give the men more time in the saddle. And it took all of the three days just to get the cattle out of the many draws and thickets. Early on the fourth day, J.W. and Alvar started their drive of the gathered cattle back to the low pasture near the headquarters.

The restless cattle took a little work to get started in the right direction, but once a big old brindle wide horned cow took the lead, the rest seemed to just follow along like a batch of kids traipsing after their grandma. On a swing back from the flank to the rear, the two men met up and at the sight of his friend the vaquero burst out laughing as J.W. stared at him with a question written across his brow in wrinkles. "What? What are you laughing about you crazy Mexican?" asked J.W.

"Oh, I was just remembering the look on Shamus face when he stuck his feet in his boots and they went squish! It was so funny I rolled back on my bed and couldn't stop laughing."

"Well, I couldn't hang around to enjoy it, but I shore heard the men laughing. Payback ain't always easy but it can be discouraging."

"Si, si, but it can also rekindle the fire. Some people can't take eet, and they think they have to always strike back. You better walk lightly my friend," warned Alvar as he reined back to chase after a stray. He waved his sombrero at his partner and continued with the drive. J.W. just shrugged his shoulders and followed the example of the vaquero. It was the tail end of dusk when they finished their drive and let their herd mix with those already gathered in the lower pasture. It had been a long four days and they both were looking forward to a big meal in the cook shack and a good night's rest in their bunks. No time was wasted as they put up the horses and gear, dropped their personal gear in the bunk house and headed for the water trough to clean up a mite before Cooky rang the dinner bell. Jake and Sean were already at the trough as J.W. and Alvar approached. Seeing the two men coming, Jake tossed the bar of lye soap to J.W. as Sean pointed out the towels hanging on the nearby fence. J.W. stripped off his hat and shirt and began splashing the water on his chest then ducked his head in the trough and came up sputtering and laughing with a "Whooeee, that feels good! I'm surprised all that dust didn't just turn to mud and settle in the bottom." With another splash of water across his chest and at his armpits, he ran his fingers through his wet hair and grabbing up the soap began to lather up. Alvar was a bit less enthusiastic about the bathing but followed the example of the others. Finishing off his cowboy bath, J.W. was putting the well-used towel to use and hearing the dinner bell, hurried up and started toward the cook shack as he was buttoning his shirt and tucking in the tail. This was the first time around the men since his prank on Shamus so J.W. chose to play his cards close to his chest.

After filling his plate, he took his usual seat beside Alvar and at the end of the bench. The others were talking about the coming branding and telling tales of other times together around the fire. Skinny asked Sean, "Say Sean, are you now the official remuda ramrod? I see you've been doin' a lot of the toppin' off of some of them new broncs we got, you gonna do that all the time?"

"Nah, everybody's gotta top off his own mount. I was just warmin' up some of the new ones for you old timers, we don't want you to be hurtin' yourselves and bein' of no use to us during the branding."

J.W. just listened as the men kidded back and forth and swapped stories both true and false of the many experiences with rank broncs, mad cows, and other varmints. All the men had spent a busy four days and didn't waste any time with cards or dice or storytelling but made their way to the bunkhouse anticipating a good night's rest. They were not to be disappointed, but J.W. did make his usual after midnight jaunt to the privy and a slight detour on his way back to his bunk. This one took him to the tack shack where the saddles and other gear were kept out of the weather. Each man knew his own gear and easily recognized the saddle of the other cowboys. Saddles were a source of pride and comfort and were often personalized with decoration or carved initials or something that would set them apart and show who owned them. Sean's was easily identified with the large silver Conchos on the black leather, and J.W. set about his chosen task.

A couple of the men were not quite asleep when they saw J.W. creep back into the bunkhouse, but they just chose to let things play out but would be careful about their own boots and bunks. They just smiled and rolled over and wondered what kind of entertainment would await them in the morning.

Chapter Eighteen

Branding

HOPPY ENTERED THE BUNKHOUSE carrying a big stick the size of his arm and the length of his leg. As he walked from bunk to bunk he smacked the end of each bunk and started yelling the same tune, "We're burnin' daylight, roll your lazy hind ends outta that bunk and quit sleepin' in like a bunch of ol' ladies! Whatdaya think this is a sewing circle! Get up and get some biscuits before Cooky throws 'em out!" His alarm was met with shouts, thrown boots and a day's worth of grumbling before he made his escape. As the men rolled from the covers, every one shook out their britches before slipping them on and banged their boot heels on the floor and held them upside down to be sure there was nothing in them. J.W. just smiled as he saw the precautions of the men and shaking his head was the first to exit the bunkhouse. The men were more relaxed and talkative after they had their first two cups of coffee and downed several biscuits, sausage, gravy and grits. All the men started out of the cook shack and sauntered toward either the bunkhouse for some of their personal gear or toward the tack shed to get their saddles and gear for the day's work at branding.

Most of the men did not have personal mounts and would take whatever was available in the corral. J.W. and Alvar would start the day with Smoke and the Andalusia, but would need to get other mounts for the last half of the day. The work during branding required a lot from the horses and it was asking too much for one horse to continually drag cows or calves to the fire and repeat it over and over again for more than half a day. Being warned the day before, the men knew they would have to top off their own mounts so they were more selective for their first horse of the day. Horses that are not used regularly begin to 'feel their oats' and are less affable with different riders. So it was common to see several riders having to take a deep seat and dig in their spurs and ride out the kinks as the horse explained his displeasure with several crow hops or a spell of bucking. Usually the men rode them out and the horses settled in for the day and worked well the rest of the ride, but occasionally there would be a bronc or two that were just plain disagreeable all day long. Each horse gained a reputation and the cowboys watched each one, catalogued his behavior, and were careful in their selection each day.

Sean had his own horse, a stout sixteen hand blood sorrel with one stocking on his front left leg, that was well known as a high spirited gelding that had bottom and could go all day if he had to. But he also was known to have a regular morning argument with his rider and this morning was no exception. J.W. and Alvar had already taken Smoke and the Andalusia out of the corral and were now busy with their tack as the horses stood hipshot at the fence. A sudden shout from one of the cowboys sitting on the top rail got their attention and they bent a little to look through the fence at the action. Sean had mounted his big sorrel and the horse was showing his displeasure as he ducked his head between his front feet and kicked at the rising sun. With the sun glinting off his horseshoes, the horse began his buck, determined to unseat his rider. Sean was good at what he knew and with boots deep in the stirrups he leaned back using his free arm for balance and stretched his legs forward to almost stand erect as he stood in his stirrups. When the big sorrel sucked back and brought up his head, he watched Sean continue over his head, saddle and all, to land on his face before the big horse. Free of his rider, the big horse sauntered to the pile of leather and flesh and sniffed at Sean as he struggled to free himself, and walked away tossing his head as if to say, "That'll show ya!" The whoops and hollers from the cowboys and brothers motivated Sean and he finally rose from the dirt, kicked at his saddle and said, "Well, I didn't get bucked off, the saddle did!" Then with a thought he began to examine his saddle. As he flipped it over, he noticed the front billet, or the leather latigo that was attached to the cinch on the right side of the saddle, was not through the D ring. There were some short pieces of twine that had apparently tied the billet to the D instead of the billet. When put under stress of the buck, the twine broke and the cinch fell free letting the saddle slide. He looked up and around the corral searching for J.W. Not seeing him, he hollered, "Where is he? I'm gonna kill him!" he shouted through clinched teeth. Immediately the rest of the men looked around for J.W. only to see their backs as J.W. and Alvar rode toward the lower pasture. With a chuckle and stepping to their chores, the men soon had the horses saddled and mounted as they followed after the prankster and his partner.

The work of branding is hard and hot. With two sets of custom made branding irons at each of the two fires, and duties assigned, the work was begun. Each fire had two men on the ground and two teams roping and dragging. The roping teams would head and heel a calf, drag it to the fire where it would be flanked to the ground and have two hind legs and a front leg tied with a piggin' string and while flat on its side would be branded. If it was a bull calf, they would try to tie the two front legs and one back leg, then stretch out the back leg while the other man cut the calf to make him a steer, then apply the brand

and release. If the calves weren't too big, one head rope would be used to drag the calf to the fire and the men would flank it down and tie it, while the other roper was busy bringing another calf. The work was more challenging when they had a maverick that was too big to flank which would require the team of ropers to bring it to the fire stretched out. If the maverick was still on its feet, one of the ground men would try to grab a free front leg and push the maverick over to its side and then sit on its neck while the heeler made sure the hind legs were stretched. The big ones still required cutting and they were not very cooperative and often required the other team to assist the ground crew until the job was done. With the stench of burning hair and flesh, dust and dirt from the roping and flanking, little time for breaks, the men were soon wiping sweat from their faces and spitting out mud balls with no time for conversation but shouted orders that added to the sometimes confusing melee.

Every hour required a rotation of duties with the ground crew mounting up and a team of ropers replacing them on the ground. It was exhausting and dirty work, but the real cowboys loved it. It was a surprise to all of them to hear the clanging of the dinner bell and they looked over to see Cooky standing at the back of a chuck wagon and clanging the triangle and smiling at the men. "Come and git it fer I throw it out!" he shouted as he turned back to his cook fire with the metal tripod holding a huge Dutch oven suspended over the fire. Grabbing a big spoon and a rag from the back of the chuck wagon, he went to the fire, moved the large blue enamel coffee pot away from the flames, lifted the lid to the Dutch oven and stepped back waiting for the first cowboy and his plate and cup.

Although a bit slow moving and each one walking like he was stove up or crippled, the cowboys made their way to the stack of plates and cups at the back of the chuck wagon and eagerly lined up to fill up. There weren't any trees to provide shade, but the first ones with plates found seats on the shady side of the chuck wagon and started slopping up the meat and potatoes and whatever else was on their plates. The biscuits disappeared along with the stew as they were used to wipe the plates clean. Upending their cups for all the coffee and even the grounds, the cowboys wiped their faces with sleeves that had dust and blood up to the elbows, but they didn't care. Before the chow line ended, a couple of men were already snoring under the chuck wagon. Florence and her dad had haltered and led eight fresh horses out to the men and the animals now stood tethered to a picket line stretched from the back wheel of the chuck wagon to a large boulder some forty feet distant. Florence hoped to get a chance to talk with J.W. but was disappointed when her dad insisted she come with him back to the house. But the men were more interested in rest than in fresh horses, and with full stomachs, the cool grass was soon littered with prone cowboys with hats over their faces and some snoring so loudly their hats bounced with the noise.

After the all-too-brief break, Patrick and Monty were the roping team while J.W. and Alvar were on ground duty. The pair on the ground soon fell into a familiar routine and worked well together. Alvar had the task of cutting and branding while the bigger J.W was tasked with flanking the calves down and tying them when necessary.

Their turn on the ground was nearing an end when Patrick and Monty shouted a warning to the ground crew. The ropers were fighting with the biggest mossy horn steer of the day. Horns that spanned five feet and upturned with fine points, a frame that held over twelve hundred pounds of determined meanness and a brindle hide that marked him as trouble, the steer tossed his head and jerked at the rope dallied to Patrick's saddle, but with both hind legs caught and held tightly together whenever he could get them under his girth, the steer was fighting what appeared to be a losing battle.

The two stout horses had all they could handle with the monster as the ground was getting turned up better than a new two bottom plow could do and the dust flying from every strike of hoof to ground both from horses and steer. With a bellow of resentment, the steer stopped his struggle and the ground crew rushed toward the beast but the big steer spotted the approaching men through blood-shot eyes and lurched toward the men. Alvar jumped back, retreated to his tethered mount and brought back a coiled blacksnake bull whip.

When the team had the brindle stretched out again, Alvar let loose his bull whip and quickly wrapped the coils around the front legs of the protesting animal, with a nod to J.W. the two men pulled together and with Patrick pulling the head the opposite way, the monster fell to his side. A quick inspection showed the animal was indeed a steer and even though previously cut, there was no evidence of a brand. With Alvar holding tightly to the bullwhip wrapped around his wrists he sat down to dig in his heels and hold the front legs of the monster.

With the legs of the animal facing the fire, J.W. snatched up the glowing branding iron, trotted around behind Monty and approached the downed steer from the back side. He raised the branding iron and brought it straight down. To make a brand clear, it is necessary to hold the brand firmly in place and if the animal moves to move with it until the brand is completely burned through the hair and onto the hide. But the steer didn't want to cooperate and J.W. had to dance with his new partner to keep from getting branded himself. Within seconds that seemed like long minutes, the job was done.

J.W. waved the iron in the air for the men to release the beast. Alvar threw his slack and let go of the bullwhip to stand ready to make his escape. Both ropers threw the slack in their ropes and spurred their mounts away, leaving J.W. exposed with nothing between him and the steer. As the animal made it to his feet, he tossed his head trying to free himself from the rope, saw J.W. and ducked his head, threw dirt over his back as he pawed the ground, and readied to charge. But by the time he looked up again, J.W. was nowhere to be found. Even J.W. didn't know he could run so fast but he flew past the fire, dropped the iron into the flames without missing a step and ran the additional hundred feet to roll under the chuck wagon. Patrick watched J.W. running and took his eyes off the steer, but the loud bellow reminded him of the danger and looking down at the approaching horns, he screamed and spurred his frightened horse away from the charge. But the steer was not so easily discouraged. He knew the man on the dapple grey was the one that started this fight and he was determined to at least even the score. Alvar started laughing to be joined by Monty as J.W. crawled out from under the wagon. They watched the dapple grey running with his tail tucked between his legs and a crazy Scotsman screaming and spurring as the big brindle steer bawled his threats that were heard by all the men at both fires. With belly laughs, hats slapping legs, and spurs jangling, the men had a good break from the monotony of the day's dirty duties.

Monty apologized to the ground crew of J.W. and Alvar as he said, "That was all Patrick. I didn't want to have anything to do with that rank ol' mossy horn, but he thought he'd teach you a lesson with that big beast. But, it looks like Patrick is the one with homework from this lesson," he chuckled as J.W. and Alvar joined in the laughter. When the day drew to a close with the coming of dusk, the weary crew stayed in the field. Their bedrolls were in the chuck wagon and after staggering through the chow line and downing their meal, it was all the men could do to find some soft grass to roll out their blankets. As the quiet settled over the tired cowboys, one man asked, "I wonder if Patrick's still runnin' from that steer." Laughter erupted from the prone forms as each one pictured the dapple grey running off into the sunset. But laughter was not enough to stay the contagion of sleep for a very tired crew.

Chapter Nineteen

Buffalo

HOPPY STOOD at the end of the table with one foot up on the bench as he leaned forward to grab his coffee cup while the men settled down and gave him their attention. "Now fellas, we're gonna need you ta' be on yore toes out yonder today. We're gonna have a Comanche Moon tonight and fer the next couple a nights and them buffalo'll probably be movin' north too. So, with the moon and them crazy Comanche follerin' the buffler, things might get a little chancy around chere. So, keep yore eyes peeled and yore rifles primed. We don't wantcha to go startin' nuthin, but if they bring it to ya, then make 'em pay. Unnerstand?" He looked from man to man to see if there were any questions before he cut the men loose for the day. With every man looking back with stoic stares, he dropped his foot to the floor with a thud and with a circular motion over his head, he dismissed the men to their duties.

Catching up their mounts and gearing up for the day, the men were in various stages of readiness around the big corral. Hoppy walked to fence where J.W. and Alvar were strapping on their saddlebags full of rations for the next few days and he said, "Fellas, you two are gonna be in the west pasture again and that's most likely where any buffler'll try to come through. Now you ain't gonna be able to stop 'em or turn 'em, so if you see 'em comin', just try to move any cattle outta the way and you two find yoreselves a hidey-hole before any o'them injuns show up. There's always been some o'them *Kotsoteka* Comanche that foller them. I 'spose that's why they're called *Buffalo eaters.* Anyway, be careful now, y'hear?" With a slap on the back of each of the men, Hoppy made his way to some of the others to see them on their way.

J.W. turned to Alvar and asked, "Uh, you know much about any of these Comanche? Are they purty bad hombres?"

"Si, senor. The only ones that are worse than the Comanche are the Apache from up around the Llano Estacado. But sometimes they get together and make raids against the ranches and villages of the plains. Mostly though, it's the Comanche. They are known for their night raids into Mexico. My family has lost many caballos to their raids. They also take captives and sell them or keep them as slaves."

"Is that what they mean by a Comanche Moon?" asked J.W.

"Si, they make their raids when there is a full moon, and because they made so many, people just call it a Comanche Moon, and they prepare for a raid."

"So, you think it's likely we'll run up against some of 'em?"

"Si, we might. But you never know about the buffalo and about the Indians. If the buffalo go some other way, maybe over by the Spear V ranch or someplace else, then we might get a good night's sleep. But if you feel the thunder, be ready."

"Feel the thunder?" asked J.W.

"Si, you will feel it before you see them."

Alvar made a slight hop, stuck his toe in the tapadero and gracefully swung astride of the anxious Andalusia. With unnoticeable knee pressure, the big black arched his neck and started to prance away from the corral. The vaquero leaned forward slightly and spoke to his horse and he stretched into a run and disappeared through the ranch gate. J.W. was still reaching for his last stirrup when Smoke jealously started after their riding partners. J.W. had to grab the saddle horn to keep from losing his seat and the others cowboys gave him a "hurrraaah" send-off.

With the branding over and the cattle dispersed to the different pastures and graze, the cowboys job was to see to the movement of the herds. To keep the grass from being over-grazed, they had to move any of the lazy bunches away from their favorite hang-outs and onto the other less grazed areas. Once the wandering herds found the newer green grass, they were easily contented and stayed where they were moved. But there were always the fool headed stubborn ones that wanted their own way, much like people, and would try to circle the cowboys to return to their previous meadow or more familiar surroundings. The ongoing contest kept the men busy and the horses tired, but by the end of the day, most of the cattle were near water and would bed down for the evening, giving the men a chance to make their own camp for the night.

One of the ravines with a spring-fed creek and some burr oak trees gave the pair a good camp for their first night out. With minimal rations and gear, they chose to dine on the leftover biscuits and thin steaks from breakfast and with the small coffeepot that Alvar was never without, they had a passable supper.

"Wal, we ain't seen hide nor hair of any buffalo, so I guess we don't need to worry about any injuns either, that right?" inquired J.W. of his more experienced partner.

"Sometimes, there are other Comanche that come down from the North hunting the buffalo, besides the Western Comanche that would follow the herd," Alvar casually remarked.

From his seat on the boulder, J.W. jumped up and asked, "Just how many of these Comanche are there, anyway?"

Alvar chuckled at the response of his young friend and answered, "The Comanche are the largest tribe of Native

Peoples in all the South West, probably the entire country. There are many bands and tribes of them. I've heard men talk about the Northern, Eastern, and Western tribes, but there are many more than that. There are so many tribes or Rancherias that even I can't remember all their names."

"Ooooeeeee, maybe I better be lightin' a shuck outta here, maybe go back to the mountains where there ain't so many of 'em. When I visited the Utes, they just said there were the Northern and the Southern Utes, and most of 'em were tolerably friendly."

"Ah, my young friend, you must understand. Indians are not so different from any other peoples, there are good ones and there are bad ones. Now these *Kotsoteka* as Hoppy called them, or the *Nokoni* - they are good people. My family has traded with them and if Peta Nocona or Lone Wanderer as he is sometimes called, is still their chief, I don't think we will have any trouble."

"You know them?" asked J.W. somewhat incredulously. Everything he had heard about the Comanche was about their war-like ways and their horse stealing and worse. The thought that his partner had traded with them and even knew some of them was a surprise.

"Si, my father and Peta Nocona have been friends for a long time. He has been in our home in Mexico."

"Well now, ain't that sumpin', here I was thinkin' we needed to be ready to go to war and you're talkin' about meetin' up with old friends. That's makes me feel a whole lot better," commented J.W. as he sat back down, picked up a stick and stirred the embers of the fire.

"But senor, we don't know which band of Indians we will see, if we see any. So, it will be best if you are very careful and as Hoppy said, keep your eyes peeled," cautioned the vaquero.

The glow of the campfire was soon replaced by the light of the rising moon. It was a sight to see as the big globe slowly climbed above the Eastern horizon. The men had rolled out their blankets with their feet pointing to the East and they now lay with hands clasped behind their heads as they watched the moon seemingly grow larger as it crawled up the black sky. Although not full, it was bright and the muted silver light provided good visibility to the men as they looked across the rolling pasture below them. The black shapes of the bedded down cows and their calves were the only blemishes on the softly lit landscape. It was a peaceful scene with the only sounds from an occasional owl asking questions of the night or a far off coyote crying for a mate.

He felt the thunder. Vibrating through the saddle that was his pillow, the growing swell of movement finally stirred the men from their deep sleep. By the position of the moon, Alvar knew it was maybe an hour or two past midnight, but there was no time to lose. Seeing J.W. rise with the unasked question on his face, Alvar said, "Come on, we've got to move those cattle!" J.W. shot up from his blankets and started saddling Smoke without realizing he was still in his union suit and nothing else. When he stepped on a sharp rock, he stumbled, grumbled and went back to his bedroll and jumped into his britches and boots. Like most cowboys, he already had his hat on and now quickly finished tightening the cinch and swung aboard the big grey.

Alvar hollered, "Let geet around them and move them back up into the draw yonder. That will put them out of the path of the buffalo! Hurry!"

At a full out run and with the men laying out on the necks of their horses with manes blowing in their faces, the two partners raced downhill from the few cattle that were now on their feet and wondering what was happening. As soon as they were below the cattle, the two started shouting and whistling to move the cows that jumped to action and started to flee the horses. Within moments the small herd of about twenty pair followed the old momma cow that headed for the cover of the tree lined ravine. The cowboys followed close behind. Once within the cover of the cluster of trees and with the cattle still moving deeper into the draw, J.W. and Alvar stopped their horses and dismounted. Taking cover behind the trees, they watched as the first of the herd appeared. The big woolies were moving at a fast walk but with so many, it appeared as a tide of brown waves rolling upon the plains. J.W. had never seen the like and he said so, but Alvar explained, "Yes, there are many. But the herds are not as big as they once were. I remember mi padre telling of herds that would take days to pass by, but no longer. There have been many buffalo hunters that take them by the hundreds just for the hides and leave the carcass to waste," he stated as he shook his head. Stepping back from the trees, he sought a seat by a bit of outcropping that provided a back rest as he sat on the soft clay soil. Both horses were ground tied and after they watched the herd pass, lost interest and were now cropping some nearby grass. Leaning against the tree, J.W. continued his vigil of the passing buffalo. As the numbers began to thin out, the sun was making its appearance behind a red band of clouds lying on the Eastern horizon. He looked at his partner and saw the man snoozing behind his sombrero with his arms folded across his chest. J.W. stretched out on the grass and tipping his hat over his eyes he joined his friend in slumber.

A short while later, Alvar stood over J.W. and nudged his foot to awaken his friend. J.W. pushed the hat back, looked at Alvar and asked, "Are they gone?"

"Si, they've been gone for some time now. We should go back to our camp and get the rest of our things. I theenk I would like some coffee, you?"

"That sounds good, maybe we can finish off them biscuits too, ya reckon?"

Back at the camp, J.W. noticed Alvar seemed to be moving a bit slower than usual but he attributed that to the uncomfortable sleeping accommodations, but he asked him, "Movin' a little slow, ain'tcha Alvar?"

"Si, si. But it is better we stay here for a while longer, so we can see if there are any Comanche following the herd. If

114

they are close, they might try for a hunt on this day, and that means they will set up their camp. It is best if we see them before they see us," he said, stating the obvious. J.W. nodded in agreement and continued with building the fire for the coffee. Alvar brought the coffee pot to the fire and set it on the flat rock nearest the flames. He was in thought about something, but J.W. chose not to push him for answers. He would share when he was ready. As the water started to boil, Alvar reached for the pot, dropped in a good handful of ground coffee beans, replaced the lid and set it back on the flat rock. He stared at the pot as he let his mind work on the problem before him. He looked up at J.W. and said, "If those Indians are following and they decide to set up camp, Senor McPherson won't be too happy. Maybe if we can talk to them and get them to set up on that bluff just past the creek, they'll be far enough away from headquarters and there won't be any problem. What do you think?"

"Uh, yeah, I spose. Course it depends on how many of 'em there are and what else they might be up to. We can't have them raidin' down to the ranch and takin' our horses, but if they ain't a gonna be doin' that, it might be alright, I reckon," agreed J.W.

With a smile on his face, Alvar reached for the pot to pour himself a cup of the thick black brew. J.W. held out his cup and received a like portion and both men leaned back against their stone backrests and savored the coffee.

Chapter Twenty

Comanche

LATE MORNING, both horses lifted their heads and pricked their ears toward the mouth of the ravine. With a hiss from Alvar, J.W. followed the vaquero up the slight bank to a rock outcropping partially obscured by a spreading juniper. They bellied down and moved to the edge to survey the plains below them. It was the beginning of the caravan of Comanche. The men watched and noted the group of warriors traveling at the head of the long column. With long hair parted in the middle and braids resting on their shoulders, all the men were bare chested or with a bone breast plate or other decoration draped from their neck. Fringed leather leggings reached to the breechcloth that was tucked under a belt and hung over the tall beaded moccasins. All had quivers full of arrows on their backs with unstrung bows sticking above the arrows. A few carried trade fusils and a couple of the men had flint locks or percussion rifles while others carried lances. There were several younger men in the group that were talking excitedly while the older men maintained their sober expressions that brokered no tom foolery from the youngsters. At a nudge from

Alvar, the two men scampered back from their perch and walked to the horses. Alvar explained, "The warrior in the front, with the scalp lock that had two feathers trailing down his back and his braids had fur woven with them, that was Peta Nocona, the friend of my father. That is good, we can talk to him."

"So, we're just gonna ride right up to 'em and start talkin'? Won't that be a little dangerous, you know, like them wantin' our scalps or sumpin'?" asked J.W.

"You just follow me and don't say anything."

"That won't be too hard. I'll probably be too scared to talk, anyway," mumbled J.W.

Alvar led the way as they walked their mounts out of the ravine and were quickly spotted by the Comanche. Three warriors started yipping the warning and started toward the two but reined up when they say the uplifted open palm of Alvar. Moving alongside the two cowboys, the Comanche warriors escorted them to the front of the cavalcade into the presence of their leader, Peta Nocona. When Alvar greeted the leader, he was immediately recognized and the two grasped forearms and smiled and started talking with considerable animation. The common language was Spanish and J.W. couldn't follow all that was said, but he did pick up on a few words and it appeared the conversation was a friendly one. With an outstretched arm, Alvar apparently was giving directions to the bluff past Crazy Woman creek and received nods from his friend. J.W. began to breathe a little easier as the conversation continued with an occasional nod toward J.W. and some additional grunts of affirmation from the chief. As the conversation seemed to come to an end, Alvar and Peta Nocona grasped forearms again, and Alvar reined his mount around followed by J.W. as the two men made their way back in the direction of their previous camp site.

As the Indian caravan moved away, Alvar began to explain to J.W. about the extended conversation. "Did you see those young men there with the others?"

"Yeah, they looked like they were pretty anxious to get a chance at my scalp."

Alvar chuckled and explained, "For a young man to become a man or a warrior, he must have a successful buffalo hunt and kill. This is the first time those young ones will have that opportunity. If they are successful, they will be honored with a feast prepared by their family and they will have a 'Give Away' dance. That's when other members of the band will throw gifts at their feet to honor them becoming a man. Those things will be used by the new warrior to establish his own lodge. So, this is a very important hunt for that band."

"O.K. but I noticed you were talking about me, what was that all about."

With another laugh, Alvar explained, "I told Peta Nocona that you were a great hunter and that you had a rifle that could shoot farther than any other. I also suggested you might help them get some buffalo and he was pleased with that. "

"You volunteered me to shoot buffalo? I ain't never shot but one of them things, and he was standin' still when I done it!" proclaimed the exasperated J.W. *That's all I need, a bunch of Indians watchin' me shoot an' what happens if I miss?* he thought to himself.

"So, when is the big hunt, tomorrow?" asked J.W.

"They will probably catch up to the herd just after mid-day, and while the women set up their tipis, the men will go on the hunt. I told Peta Nocona we'd be along shortly and join up with them."

J.W. and Alvar watched with interest as the warriors readied their fresh horses that would be used for the hunt. Most of the men had several horses and had a favorite for hunting buffalo. The big bison would easily spook a high spirited animal that wasn't familiar with the beasts and put the rider in danger of being thrown and trampled. The hunters preferred a fast mount that would willingly run alongside the beast to give the warrior a good chance at making a kill. Some mounts had a preference of right side or left. Those that willingly ran along the right side, would be used by those hunting with bows and arrows or a lance. While the left runners would be used by a hunter that was left handed and could shoot to the right. These were proven hunters chosen by the warriors. Some of the horses were decorated with paint or had feathers woven into the mane but most were simply outfitted with the rawhide saddles used by the Comanche.

Alvar and Peta discussed the plan for the hunt and it was agreed that J.W. would take position at a promontory on the near side of the herd. The mounted hunters would start their hunt from the rear and the far side of the herd, giving J.W. clear shooting from his position. It took a bit of arguing to convince the chief that J.W. could take a buffalo from that distance which was between two and three hundred yards, but he finally relented, thinking that all white men were a bit crazy anyway. Alvar explained the plan to J.W. and the two men took the promontory together. Within a quarter hour, the rest of the hunters were in position and started their hunt. As was their custom, they charged the herd as if they were on the warpath and the sudden noise startled the herd and they began moving away from the nuisance. The younger hunters that were on their manhood quest were allowed to lead the charge and they were not at a loss for enthusiasm and eagerness. The older warriors followed but were quickly involved in the hunt and a few of the animals began falling.

On the promontory, J.W. took a kneeling position, laying his paper cartridges and caps handily nearby. He used his left knee as his elbow rest and sighted in on a big bull at the edge of the herd. He just wanted to calculate distance and set his sight for the determined range. He was ready and waiting when the Comanche started the herd moving with their charge. As the startled animals raised their heads, J.W. squeezed off his first shot. A young bull dropped as if his legs were pulled out from under him. Alvar slapped his friend on the shoulder and said, "Yes, you got heem! Good shooting, my friend!" But J.W. didn't pause to accept the accolades and quickly flipped open the breech ejecting the remains of the paper cartridge, inserted another, closed the breech and placed a cap on the nipple, cocked the hammer and set the rear trigger. Taking aim at a slow moving cow, he started to squeeze but a rust colored calf ran alongside so he swung the muzzle back to take aim at another bull. His shot found its mark as a puff of dust flared from the short neck just behind his massive head, a puff that could be seen even amidst the beginnings of the stampede stirred dust cloud. The head of the beast dropped and he buried his nose in the grass and slid another ten feet before coming to a stop on his belly with legs tucked under his mass. The shooting scene was repeated four more times as the herd moved past the promontory. The carcasses of six animals littered the grass to the side of the thundering herd.

Suddenly Alvar slapped his shoulder and shouted, "Look, there where the paint horse is! That's one of the young hunters!" Standing with his rein in his hand, the young man was searching the ground for something while behind him the herd seemed to be widening and several massive brown heads with blood shot eyes were coming on the hunter. "He doesn't see them! They will keel heem!" J.W. swung back to try to take aim at the charging bulls, and saw the young man's horse spook, jerk the rein from the hand of his rider and run away from the charging herd. The young man started to run in the direction of the promontory but it was evident the charging bulls would be too fast. J.W. squeezed off a shot and the lead bull had dropped his head for the charge but hit the dirt causing the beast to do an end over end somersault with his almost two thousand pounds coming down amidst the thunder. The huge carcass caused the others to veer to the side with two stumbling and falling causing a collision with others. The pile up of monsters gave just enough time to the fleeing young man to make good his escape. He dropped behind a large boulder and gasping for air, he dared not look at the passing herd of buffalo.

J.W. sat up and leaned back against a nearby boulder and said, "That was close. Ya think that's enough meat for 'em?" he asked Alvar. The vaquero nodded his head as a broad smile split his face. "Si, I theenk they will be happy with the extra meat. You did good senor," he said as he patted his friend on the back again. Alvar stood and waved at the young man to join them. With a tentative look around, the young man sprinted to the side of the vaquero and asked in Spanish, "Did you shoot that bull?" referring to the one that fell and saved his life.

"No, no, my friend did that," he said as he motioned to J.W.

The young man looked at J.W. and turned to look at the boulder he used for a refuge, then at the trampled grass where the herd passed and the carcass of the big bull. There was another carcass next to it, apparently one of the fallen animals broke its neck in the clash of colossals. He looked at the distance, back at J.W. and again at the carcasses. "You mean he shot that bull from here? That is a long way!"

Although J.W. didn't understand the words, he thought he knew what was said and smiled at the boy's response. Alvar also chuckled, and nodded in the affirmative. The young man shook his head and started to walk away. Alvar quickly stopped him and suggested he wait and the two men would help him find his mount.

After retrieving the boy's horse, the men returned to the site of the hunt. J.W. was surprised to see every carcass with several women and young people busily working to dress out the animals. He knew the people would use every possible part of the animals and when they were finished, there would be little left for the coyotes that were already prowling the perimeter. By nightfall, everyone was back in the camp and cook fires were blazing with meat being prepared for the feasts. Usually there would be several small feasts, but because of the special occasion and the events of the day, Peta Nocona had determined there would be one large feast for the village and the dance for the new warriors would include all that participated.

J.W. and Alvar were both honored and treated to special cuts and treats from the feast. The story of the lifesaving shot from the 'far shooting rifle' and the new friend of the people was told by the young man. Although slightly embarrassed because he lost his bow and had stopped to retrieve it, he nevertheless gave honor to J.W. for saving his life. With the feast and dancing going on without any sign of ending anytime soon, both J.W. and Alvar excused themselves and left to return to their camp.

"Well, that was quite a day. Those are good people, Alvar. You were right about that," stated J.W. as he reflected on the hunt and the reception they received at the feast.

"Yes, but they can also be very bad enemies. It is best to have them as friends."

"Whatdoya think ol' man McPherson'll say about them settin' up their camp where they are?"

"He has often said he doesn't like Indians of any kind. I think in years past; he has had to fight them many times. I theenk he had some family killed or wounded, but he doesn't like them."

"Are we gonna tell him about 'em?" inquired J.W. yielding to the experience and judgment of the vaquero. J.W. knew that sometimes it was best to keep quiet about some things until the circumstance provided a better opportunity, but he was never one to lie or shy away from the truth. Although the Comanche had a lot more warriors than McPherson had cowhands, the McPherson crew could do a lot of damage to a people that were just trying to survive.

"We will only answer if he questions us, and you let me do the explaining. O.K.?"

"That's fine with me, you can rope that calf all by yourself."

Chapter Twenty-One

Confrontation

J.W. AND ALVAR WERE surprised when James Enoch McPherson followed them to the corral as they were preparing to start another day's work. Usually the only time the hands saw the owner was if he was sitting on the porch when they came in from the day's work with the cattle or on special occasions like the branding. He usually dictated his orders to Hoppy and let the ramrod pass it on to the men. More often, he just let Hoppy run things and seldom interfered. So when he was out and about this early they thought something was wrong or some changes were going to be made. And when he approached them, J.W. and Alvar guessed it had something to do with the Indians and the buffalo.

"So, Shamus and Jake said they saw where a good-sized herd of buffalo passed through the West pasture the other day, and that's where you two were working. Do you have something you need to tell me?" said James Enoch, addressing himself mostly to Alvar but including J.W. in the question.

"Not much to tell senor, Hoppy told us to be on the lookout for theem and we were. We pushed the cattle up into the draws so they wouldn't get caught up with theem, and we lost none of theem. So, what's to tell?" asked the vaquero innocently.

"Were there any Indians followin' them?" queried the Scotsman.

"We watched for a long time after the buffalo passed, a really long time, and we saw no Indians following closely behind the herd."

"What about you, J.W.?" asked James Enoch of the lanky cowboy as he reached for his saddle.

"Uh, yeah, what he said," answered J.W. as he gestured toward Alvar.

The big Scotsman looked from one to the other obviously suspecting something but not able to discern exactly what and turned to leave. But the vaquero stopped him with, "But we did see some later."

Whirling back around with a flush coloring his face, he snarled from clenched teeth, "You saw some Indians and didn't tell us? Did you kill any of them?"

"No, we didn't keel them. We talked to them," answered Alvar quietly.

"Talked to them? You talked to them? What are you some kind of Indian lover?" barked the man through his bushy red beard that bounced with every word.

"Si, si. I know the leader, Peta Nocona, he is a friend of my family. We have traded with heem and his people."

"I don't want you to talk to 'em or trade with 'em, I want you to kill them!" he declared.

"But senor, they had over thirty warriors and there were just two of us. It was best for us to talk and help them get the buffalo. That way they would not take any of your cows or horses. They are good people," explained Alvar without apology. Alvar was a man that had no back-up in him, he knew he was right and would not abide any wrong doing.

"Well, that's just great! Now we've got two Injun lovers on the place, that's great!" the old man grumbled as he stomped back to the main house. Florence was standing on the veranda and watched the entire confrontation and waited for her father to return. She leaned against the rail and when her father ducked his head to mutter to himself, she threw a kiss to J.W. and smiled broadly as she watched him swing the saddle atop his big grey. She waved as she turned to follow her father back into the house.

The two men spent the morning in the South end of the pasture checking on the cattle and moving some to different areas. The passing buffalo herd had left their mark with a wide swath of pasture grass either eaten down or trodden under. Two thousand plus of the big woolies were a moving mass of destruction, and they had left their mark on the large pasture area. But nature has a way of restoring itself, with the turning of the soil and the mobile fertilizer spreader, the pasture would come back within five to six weeks and would be greener than ever. In the meantime, it fell on the men to keep the cattle rotating grazing areas to keep from eating the grasses down beyond its ability to restore itself.

Shortly after their nooning, the men agreed to make a quick visit to the Comanche and caution them about the McPhersons and the old man's hatred of any Indians. As they approached the village, J.W. was surprised at the industriousness of the people. The women were busy with the staked out buffalo hides, scraping the remaining flesh and preparing them for the next step in the tanning process. Young women were busy slicing the meat into long thin strips and hanging them on the drying racks, and the boys were gathering firewood to make the smoke fires for smoking the meat and curing the hides. Some of the men were working on shaping new arrows, putting on the fletching, and knapping the flint arrowheads. Others were working on fashioning water containers from the stomachs of the buffalo while some of the men were using the rawhide to braid ropes or make shields. Everyone was busy except for a few grey headed men that were gathered around a central fire and leaning back on willow back rests. J.W. correctly assumed these were the revered elders that had earned their leisure and were enjoying the time together of sharing old war stories and more. It was a pleasing sight and just observing the people busy at life gave J.W. a sense of camaraderie with them.

Alvar spoke with his friend while J.W. walked casually through the camp observing the people. Those that noticed him were cordial in their greetings but did not stop their work. He continued on his stroll and noticed a few of the new warriors had gathered around one of the lodges and were busily making war clubs and discussing their plans for the future. Although he didn't understand the language, he understood the expressions and repartee and easily discerned that some of the young women were the topic of discussion. He smiled and passed on. Returning to where he left Alvar, he saw the vaquero motioning him that it was time to leave. He joined his friend and they soon left the camp. J.W. asked, "So, what'd he think about McPherson maybe payin' him a visit?"

"Ah, he ees not worried. He has plenty of warriors and they are always careful. He also said they weel be leaving soon, maybe even before the McPhersons try anything. It will be O.K., I'm thinking."

"Well, I hope so, I'd hate to see anything happen to 'em. Like you said, they're good people."

"Si, si. Peta told me he was one of the chiefs that signed the Fort Scott treaty and they would keep it, no matter what McPherson does. Also, you will be glad to know that he said the soldiers promised a Christian preacher was going to come and help them and maybe teach their children in a school."

"Really? Hey, that's great news. My Pa would have liked that. That's what he felt God was calling him to do before the Pawnee hit the wagon train and killed him and the others," he dropped his head as the memories flooded in but continued, ". . . yeah, that's great. I sure hope whoever it is does a good job."

Alvar looked at his friend and asked, "Why don't you do eet? You would be a good teacher for theem."

J.W. looked back at his friend and replied, "Nah, I can teach a bit of school, but doing the preacher thing, that's a calling and God hasn't been talking to me about nothin' like that," he stated with relief showing on his face.

After putting up their horses, the two men started toward the cook shack having heard Cooky and his clanging triangle as they came back into the headquarters grounds. Monty exited from the bunkhouse and caught up with them before they reached the cook shack and said, "You fellas better be careful. Since Patrick found out about you two talkin' to the Indians, he's takin' up the warpath his own self and he's spoilin' for a fight. Just sayin'."

After filling their plates, they took the familiar seats across the table from the brothers and started into their meal. The rest of the men at the table busied themselves with their rations but conversation was non-existent and the mood of the room was one of expectancy. J.W. guessed the rest of the men knew the plans of the brothers and were staying out of the pending confrontation. They didn't have long to wait. As expected, Patrick was the one to open the dance. He wiped his plate with the last bite of biscuit, moved his plate aside while he chewed the last bite, then said, "Cooky, either your cookin' is gettin' worse, or the stink of Injun lovers is ruinin' all your hard work. Don't you agree boys?" The only agreeing came from his brothers but they just nodded their heads. It was easy to see they were not happy with the actions of their brother, but neither would they step in to prevent anything.

"I said, don't you agree boys?" he said with a raised voice and a finger pointing at J.W. expecting him to agree. But J.W. just kept forking in his supper and acted as if he didn't hear the taunts of the bully. "You stinking Injun lovers! I'm sick of you and all your nonsense and I'm tired of you hanging around my sister! You hear me greenhorn?" he shouted at J.W. as he leaned across the table and pounded his fist making the plates and cups bounce.

J.W. leaned back and looked straight at Patrick and quietly said, "If you don't like it here, you can always leave."

The suggestion enraged the already angered Patrick and as he stood up he grabbed the edge of the table and upended it onto the laps and chests of the five men on that side. The sudden action pushed the men and their bench over causing a pile up of men, table, bench and the utensils and leftovers of the supper. As they tumbled to their backs amidst the mess, there was a tangle of arms and legs as each one fought to free himself of the stuff. As the men still seated rose to separate themselves from the melee, Patrick roared as he kicked back at the remaining bench and grabbed at a leg of the table to rip it free with the thought of using it as a club against his adversary. Within moments, the men under the table freed themselves and were standing and wiping the remains of the meal from their chests and britches when Patrick roared and swung at J.W.'s head. The target of his wrath ducked the blow and answered with a round house right to Patrick's jaw that set him back on his heels giving J.W. time to free himself from the entanglement of the now broken cook shack furniture. The rest of the men fled through the open door except for Alvar and Monty that stayed behind.

Regaining his balance, a now more careful Patrick began to move side to side slapping the table leg in his open hand and scowling at J.W. With an air of nonchalance, J.W. just moved his upper body to counter the threats of Patrick. With another roar and a charge with uplifted table leg, Patrick began his swing down toward J.W.'s head, but the young man didn't wait for the blow but instead lowered his shoulder and charged under the swing. Taking Patrick in the gut with his shoulder, he drove the man the length of the cook shack and flattened him against the wall driving the air from his lungs. As J.W. backed away, Patrick bent over sucking air to get his wind back. Bracing his legs, J.W. brought his fist from the floor and connected with the face of Patrick, smashing his nose as the blood spurted in all directions. The impact straightened the

Scotsman to his toes and he wasn't prepared for the flurry of fists to his waist that pushed him back against the wall. With no room to absorb the impact the big Scotsman was pummeled between the wall and the pounding fists from the greenhorn. With his eyes rolling back in his head, Patrick slid to the floor in a heap and lay still. J.W. watched to see if he was breathing, grabbed his shoulder to roll him on his back and with his hands under his armpits pulled the man from the cook shack. Dragging him to the water trough, J.W. used his cupped hands to splash water on the face of Patrick to revive him. With a sputter and a cough, the would-be assailant rolled to his side to spit out two teeth and coughed some more. Looking up at J.W. he threatened, "This ain't over."

J.W. shook his head and walked back to the bunkhouse. He picked up his riata from his bunk and started his nightly round of rope therapy as he walked toward the barn. As he turned the corner he was surprised to see Flo waiting for him. Lifting his eyebrows in a question, she responded, "Sean came in and told us what was happening. I knew you'd whip him, I just wish it was me. He's had it coming for a long time now."

"I didn't want to do it, but he left me no choice, especially when he threatened me with not being able to see you. You're the only reason I'm still here Flo, you know that don't you?"

"I know, and I'm glad you're still here. I couldn't stand it if I couldn't see you." She continued to walk beside him and paused, looked at him and said, "I think I'm falling in love with you, J.W."

He looked at her with a somber expression and said, "Not me."

Surprised, she stopped and grabbed his arm to turn him, "What do you mean, not you? You mean you don't love me?" she asked fearfully.

"I mean, not me, I don't think I'm falling in love with you," he paused watching her response, and continued, "I know I'm in love with you. I don't have to think about it, I know."

Letting a smile slowly cross his face he watched his sweetheart when she clasped both hands to her mouth and with a sparkle in her eyes tiptoe and kiss him full on the mouth while he stood with hands full of riata and surprise.

Chapter Twenty-Two

Blame

THE COOK SHACK was unusually quiet with the brothers absent. The conversation was muted and minimal as the men focused on the usual biscuits and gravy and thin sliced steaks. The coffee was hot and strong and the men leisurely savored the meal. Hoppy stepped into the room and announced, "Fellas, I know this is Sunday an' yore used to lazin' around on yore day off, but the boss has a cattle buyer up from San Antone and you'll be needed to move some stock around, cepin' you J.W. Yore 'sposed to go on into yore schoolin' wid' da ladies. Now fer the rest of ya' go 'head on an' finish yore vittles and I'll catch up wit' ya' at the corral." He turned and left in a hurry with other responsibilities pulling him away. It wasn't unusual for the boss to ask them to work on their day off, but like people everywhere, the cowboys grumbled about it. J.W. cleaned his plate with the last bit of biscuit, popped the soppy biscuit in his mouth and stood to leave. Monty said, "Wait up, J.W., I'll go with you."

As they walked to the bunkhouse, Monty spoke, "J.W., ya' need to be extra careful. I heard Patrick talkin' with his brothers last night and he's madder'n an old wet hen. He's determined he's gonna get even with you if'n it's the last thing he does. I wouldn't put anything past him, y'hear?"

"Yeah, I hear ya', I just wish he'd leave it alone. What else could I do? Just let him whip me? That ain't the way I was brought up. My Pa, even though he was a preacher, always said to stand up for myself and for what's right."

"Oh, I agree with you, J.W., but Patrick's only thinkin' about the drubbin' you gave him. He's always been able to bully his way 'round, and he ain't likin' it at all. So, just watch yore step."

"I will, Monty, and thanks," replied J.W. as Monty headed for his bunk and his gear. J.W. grabbed up his rifle and scabbard, saddle bags, and with a pause and a thought, rolled up his bedroll with his change of clothes and tucked it under his arm as he left the bunkhouse. Retrieving his saddle and other gear from the tack shed, J.W. was soon ready to head into town. He was surprised to see Florence drive the team and wagon from the barn with her mother in the seat beside her. "Nobody else comin'?" he asked.

"Nope, it's just us today. Pa and the boys are caterin' to that cattle buyer so we're on our own," replied Flo with a conspiratorial smile. J.W. smiled back as he gigged his horse to follow the buckboard. He wasn't sure what plans Flo had for the day, but he was willing to follow her lead. *She's never steered me wrong before!* he thought.

Jesse Chisholm was the cattle buyer from San Antone. Well known in the area as an interpreter for the Indians with his knowledge of the Comanche, Kiowa, and Apache languages, Chisholm was also known for his many years in the area fighting Mexicans, Indians and outlaws. Sometimes contracted by the army to provide beef for the seven army posts established after the Mexican war to protect the settlers, he was on a buying tour to fill the army's orders and others for the needs of San Antonio. This was his first time at the McPherson ranch and the big Scotsman was determined to impress the buyer with their large herd and ability to provide the required beef.

The early part of the morning was spent riding through the nearby meadows and inspecting the readily visible cattle. McPherson had dispatched his cowboys on a mission to move as many cattle down into the easily accessible grassy meadows before he followed with the buyer. "Well, James Enoch, I'm impressed! You have a good sized herd and they're all lookin' fat and sassy, I'd say. If we come to a deal, will you be able to drive the herd to San Antone?"

"Aye, we can do that. I've got me a good bunch of cowboys and we can get them to wherever you'd want them, easy enough," assured McPherson.

"Well, they won't all have to go to San Antone, you might drop some off at Fort Groghan and Fort Scott, but we'll have to see how many we can agree on."

James Enoch smiled at the thought of a good sale of cattle. It had been several years of building up his herd with very little return and the thought of finally realizing some profit for the years of hard work was very pleasing. By late morning, Chisholm said he'd seen enough and was anxious to wrap things up so the two men turned back toward the headquarters. McPherson waved his hat at the men by the herd to let them know their work was finished and the cowboys followed the boss and the buyer back to the house. Senora Alvarez, the cook for the main house, had prepared a fine dinner for all the McPhersons and their guest. Using the water on the washstand beside the house, the men washed up and were soon seated around the feast. Without the women present, the men chose to forego the usual blessing and dove into their meal. With conversation focused on the number of cattle needed and the current market price, the brothers were more intent on feeding their face than their bank account. At the conclusion of the meal, James Enoch suggested they retire to the veranda for a cigar and finish the deal.

The brothers stood leaning against the veranda railing while the buyer took a seat in one of the two rockers when James Enoch excused himself for a visit to the privy. Shamus asked Chisholm about his years fighting the Mexicans and the buyer was glad to regale the brothers with his tales. As the four men enjoyed a bit of laughter over one of the escapades, they were startled by a shout from their father. "Help! Help me! Git out here you lazy whelps and git me outta here!" he yelled. The brothers ran to the privy and grabbed the door pulling it open to see the bottom of their father's feet and his head over his knees. The seat of the privy had split in two and dropped the man into the divide and he was suspended by his heels and his outstretched arms. The split in the seat was wedged in such a way that as he tried to lift himself up, the ragged edges of the wood poked into his thighs and hips and prevented his escape.

The brothers crowded the door to look at the embarrassed man and struggled to stifle a laugh to be stopped by, "It ain't funny! Now get me outta here!" he demanded. Shamus gave the orders and instructed Patrick and Sean to, "Push down on the ends of them boards while I pull him out." It was easier said than done for three sizable brothers to crowd into the two seater privy and work around one another, but within a short while, they successfully rescued their distraught father. All the while they worked the big redhead grumbled and threatened, and as he stood pulling up his britches, he turned to look at the damage. Patrick was the first to exclaim, "I bet that greenhorn had somethin' to do with this!"

"What do you mean?" demanded James Enoch.

"Well, he's the one that's done everthing else! I betcha he made this so it'd break, too!"

As James Enoch examined the broken boards, he said, "Maybe, he mighta pushed 'em so they'd split, but I dunno."

Patrick leaned in to look at the ends of the boards at the edge of the platform, pointed and said, "Lookee here, I think them scratches are from him loosening them nails so the pot'd drop!"

James Enoch leaned to look but couldn't see much in the dim light. Yielding to the demands of his oldest son and wanting to punish someone or something for his embarrassment, he let his anger boil and said, "Maybe you're right! He needs to be taught a lesson!"

"But Pa, we don't know that for sure, we can't go runnin' off after him if we don't know, especially with them at church," pleaded Sean, knowing it was Patrick's goading that was driving the need for vengeance.

"Get the horses! We're goin' after him," ordered the old man.

The pastor's text for his sermon was taken from Matthew 5:38-39, *Ye have heard that it hath been said, An eye for an eye, and a tooth for a tooth. But I say unto you, "That ye resist not evil: but whosoever shall smite thee on thy right cheek, turn to the other also."* The sermon was the topic of conversation during the after service meal on the grounds. J.W. asked Flo, "So, how does that apply to the problem with your brothers?"

"J.W., everything that's happened, my brothers started. But maybe you shouldn't have retaliated with so many of your pranks . . . but they were funny," she giggled.

"I've tried several times to get Patrick to end it, but he keeps promising, 'It's not over'."

"I know. Maybe God's just testing your patience," she consoled as she jumped down from her seat on the tailgate of the buckboard. "Come on, we've got to get school set up for the kids." She extended her hand to him and they walked hand in hand to the steps of the church. As they started up the steps, they heard the clatter of hooves on the roadway and an increase in the level of conversation from the remaining crowd at the table. The couple turned around to see what the disturbance was about and saw James Enoch McPherson and the boys galloping up to the church grounds on lathered up horses. James Enoch spotted his daughter and J.W. on the steps and as he slid his horse to a stop he hollered, "You, J.W., stop where you are!"

Florence was behind J.W. and a step above him. She moved closer to her right and grabbed the hand rail as she knew her father and her brothers and she knew this was not good. It wasn't often she saw her father angry but his red cheeks glared from over his beard and the fire in his eyes could have lit a dark room. The brothers followed their father as the four men stomped by the tables and confronted the man on the steps. A distance of about thirty feet separated the men and James Enoch said, "We've had enough of your nonsense! What you did to my privy cuts it! I ain't gonna have no more of it, you understand?"

"Uh, nosir I don't. I don't know anything about your privy or whatever it is that's got you so upset," he denied.

Patrick piped in with, "We know you done it! I told you this weren't over!" he shouted.

J.W. raised his hands with open palms and said, "Honest, I don't know what you're talkin' about. Whatever it was, it wasn't me that done it!"

Patrick wouldn't let this pass and drew his revolver. J.W. remained with his hands up and empty. With anger pulling the trigger, Patrick's pistol blasted causing everyone at the tables to jump off their seats and one old lady to faint. The bullet passed through the forearm of J.W. and spun him sideways. He grabbed at his arm as blood spilled on the railing and through his fingers. He turned to face the men, saw Patrick cocking his pistol and taking aim and J.W. was forced to draw his Navy Colt and fire. With his natural aim and quick reflexes, he triggered two rounds that blossomed red on the chest of Patrick, knocking him back and flat on his back. The old man and brothers turned to the prone form and the old man dropped to his knees cradling the head of his oldest son in his arms. His mother, Rebecca, rushed to the side of her son trying in vain to catch her breath as she held a small hanky to her mouth.

Florence saw the blood coming from J.W.'s arm, looked at her family gathered around Patrick and said to J.W., "You better leave, hurry!" With a glance at the crowd, J.W. vaulted from the steps and hurried around to the back of the church to the lean-to stables where he had tethered Smoke. Florence caught up with him as he mounted and with a hand on his leg said, "Go to Waxahachie, you'll be safe there and I'll try to get word to you, but whatever you do, come back to me!" she instructed with tears streaming down her freckled face.

"I will, I will. Somehow, this'll all work out and I'll come back for you." Spurring Smoke, he left nothing else behind but a cloud of dust. And once again, he was riding lonesome.

Chapter Twenty-Three

Frustration

HE SPURRED THE BIG GREY into a ground eating lope as he leaned down on the neck of his faithful Smoke and spoke to his only companion, "Come'on boy, we gotta get outta here. That cantankerous old man's liable to mount a posse or sumpin' and we need to be long gone 'fore that happens." He reached down and patted the neck of Smoke as the black mane whipped at his face. He didn't have a plan on what to do although Florence told him to go to Waxahachie. All J.W. knew was Waxahachie was North and that's the direction they were headed. The flat and sometimes rolling plains before them stretched out with a monotonous green and brown with the Indian and Buffalo grass waving at his passing. They covered just over a mile and the long legged grey was still stretching out without any slowing to his pace. But the lather was showing on his withers and neck and J.W. pulled up on the reins to give Smoke a bit of a breather. Walking and sucking wind, the faithful mount still covered ground as they sighted a line of thick trees that meant water. The stately Oak and Sassafras were mixed with Elm and Cottonwood and a few other unfamiliar leafy trees that J.W. couldn't identify, but the shady cluster of trees was a welcome sight. As they entered the shade following an old game trail, they quickly came to the bank of a river. Speaking to his only friend, J.W. said, "Well, Smoke ol' buddy, I don't know what the name of this here river is, but I don't rightly care. We both need a break 'fore we go any further and I'm thinkin' you could use a good long drink." As they approached the stream on a bit of a sandbar, J.W. dropped the reins to remove his hat and wipe the sweat from his forehead. Smoke didn't hesitate and walked straight into the water until he was knee deep then stuck his nose down, snorted and began his long drink. "Whoa now boy, take it easy," said J.W. as he reached for the floating rein to pull his horse back to the sandbar. "We don't want you to get too much and have it puttin' you in a hurt. Just hold on there, we'll get more in a bit. Come on with me and let's get you some nice green grass in the shade. We still got a ways to go 'fore we make camp."

Rebecca looked at her husband and back to her son. Patrick's eyes stared at the sun and his chest was still. Blood pooled beside him and touched the edge of his mother's dress. She hastily pulled her pale blue skirt back, struggled to get up, stumbled to a nearby bench and sat at the table. Looking back at her family gathered around Patrick, she dropped her face to her arms on the table and sobbed. The ladies at the table gathered around her, put their hands on her shoulders and just let their presence be known. There was nothing they could say to a mother that just lost her first born.

"Where is he?" roared the big bearded Scotsman. The brothers fell back away from the big man as he stood to his feet looking around for J.W. "I'm gonna kill him!"

"Pa, you can't, he's gone, 'sides Patrick shot him first. You can't kill him!" declared Sean trying to calm his father. But James Enoch just pushed Sean aside as he stomped into the church in search of J.W. He quickly came back out and stood

139

on the steps looking around. He stormed around the side of the church and almost knocked Florence over. He grabbed her by both arms and shook her and said, "Where is he?"

"He's gone Pa. He left 'cause I told him to!"

"You told him to? What about your brother? He's lying dead over there and you told his killer to leave!" He cocked back his arm ready to strike his daughter but his wife grabbed the arm and hissed, "Don't you dare strike our daughter!"

He looked at his wife and back at his daughter and slowly sobered, relaxed his grip on her arm and said, "I . . .I . . .I'm sorry lassie. I just lost my mind. I didn't mean nothin' by it."

"I know Pa, I know," replied Florence.

"Now you listen to me, James Enoch McPherson, you and I both know that you and Patrick brought this on and that boy was just defending himself," she started but the big man raised his head and anger flared in his eyes, but she continued, "and we've got a son to bury. And you've got a cattle buyer back at the ranch and from what the boys say you've committed to a cattle drive. Now, let's get busy with what we've got to do," she stated with the firmness that only a strong woman could exude. As the one that gave birth to the boy, she was hurting even more than her husband but she didn't have the liberty to indulge anger and she wasn't about to lose any more of her family to this nonsense of retribution.

While he watched Smoke cropping the grass, J.W. reloaded his pistol. It wouldn't do to run into some unfriendly Indians and not be ready for whatever came. He was also thinking about the McPhersons and thought they might already be in pursuit. He stomped his foot at the ground and thought, *Why'd he have to shoot? That was plumb uncalled for and I didn't want to shoot him, but he was gettin' ready to drill me and I couldn't just stand there and let him kill me. I know that's not what the pastor was sayin' in his sermon. I figger I'd already turned the other cheek, but that blasted Patrick kept after me!* His frustration brought him to his feet and he walked to Smoke, picked up the trailing reins and said, "All right boy, guess we better put some distance between us and them."

With the shading light of dusk, J.W. spotted a copse of trees away from the roadway that would make a good camp and reined his horse to the welcoming glen. Dropping the saddle to the ground, he slipped the halter over Smokes head and used the long lead to tether the horse by a patch of tall grass. J.W. realized he didn't have any supplies except what little was packed in his saddle bags, some strips of smoked meat, a bit of pemmican, a little bit of salt and some coffee beans. Without a coffee pot, the beans were useless, but he would make do. As he turned to look for a spot for his bedroll, a curious rabbit hopped from one bush toward another, but J.W. was quick to draw and shoot. The .36 caliber round flipped the rabbit end over end and J.W. hurried to claim his prize. As he examined the carcass he thought, *Well, thank you Lord for providin' my supper. Shore is a shame to shoot this harmless creature, but it's gonna taste mighty good to this hungry outlaw. Yeah, that's what I am, I guess, an outlaw. Don't like the sound of that.*

It was late afternoon when J.W. rode into the outskirts of Waxahachie. Spotting a livery, he reined his horse toward the big barn like structure with a hay mow over the wide door. Painted across the front of the building was a sign announcing the business as a livery and blacksmith. A sizable man with a leather apron and a hammer in his hand greeted J.W. as he stepped down from his saddle. "Howdy friend, need to put yore horse up?" he asked.

"Yeah, I do, and if you got a spare stall or room in your loft, I'd admire bein' able to throw out my bedroll," replied J.W.

"Shore, shore, that'll work. Just put yore horse in that stall over thar," he motioned with the hammer, "and you can bunk up in the loft." He motioned with his head and eyes to the overhead loft that beckoned the weary rider. "It'll be fifty cents a day for the both of ya."

J.W. reached into his pocket, brought out three dollars and handed it to the smithy. "I'm not sure how long I'll be stayin' but that'll take care of most of a week, if that's all right."

The broad smile of the big man showed his approval as he returned to the anvil mounted on the stump near his forge. He was working on a horseshoe and motioned with the tongs over his shoulder, "Just down the walk yonder's a purty good place to eat, Milly puts out a real good spread, if'n yore hungry." The thought of a good meal stirred his hunger and J.W. quickly finished rubbing down the grey, putting some oats in the feed bin, and with a pat on the rump said, "I'll be back ol' boy. Enjoy your supper."

Milly didn't disappoint, his plate was full to overflowing. A big slice of roast beef, a pile of potatoes and carrots smothered in rich brown gravy, two big rolls and a big mug of steaming coffee brought a smile to the lanky and hungry cowboy. He smiled up at Milly as she stood back to see if he needed anything else and said, "Now you be sure to save some room for a big slice of fresh apple pie, y'hear?"

He smiled again as he laughed and responded, "I'll always have room for apple pie, why that's my favorite!" declared J.W. Milly stood with hands on ample hips and smiled as she responded, "Yeah, an' I bet if all I had was cherry pie, that'd be yore favorite too, wouldn't it?"

"Yes mam, it sure would. My Ma taught me to appreciate the labor of a good woman in the kitchen. She said the best way to show you appreciate what they've done, is to clean your plate and share a smile," he said as he flashed another broad smile at the big woman. She dropped her hands and as she turned away said, "Oh go on with you now, you sweet talkin' devil!" J.W. just chuckled and dug into the good smelling vittles.

J.W. stretched his legs with a walk down the boardwalk of the town. The main street was lined with a variety of businesses typical of every small town in the growing frontier. There were two saloons, one mercantile, a lady's dress shop, a gun shop, a lawyer, and two other storefronts that were boarded up and had no identifying signs. J.W. just assumed they were businesses that didn't make it and continued on his stroll. Returning to the livery, he started to check on Smoke when he noticed another man tending to his horse across the way from Smoke. The man spoke first with, "Evenin'."

J.W. responded with, "Howdy."

"You know your way around town?" asked the stranger.

"Ain't much to the town, but I just got in a while ago. Lookin' for somethin' special?"

"Just a place to eat, the smithy was gone when I came in so you're the first one I could ask," commented the stranger leaving the question hanging.

"Well, Milly put out a good spread for me. Her place is just a couple doors down the boardwalk yonder."

The man had finished tending his mount and now approached J.W. with an extended hand as he introduced himself, "I'm Captain J.B. McGown of the Texas Mounted Volunteers, and you're . . .?" The Texas Mounted Volunteers would later be known as the Texas Rangers but were now made up of volunteers and a few paid officers that were concerned about the lawlessness and Indian problems throughout the new state.

"Uh, John Harpold, but most folks call me J.W." answered J.W. as he grasped the man's hand.

"Well, J.W., I'd buy you a cup o' coffee, if you're of a mind to join me," offered McGown. Not wanting to stir up any suspicion, J.W. accepted the offer and the two men started for Milly's place. As they were seated, J.W. asked, "So, just what are the Mounted Volunteers?"

"Well, with the growing population and the new statehood, the governor was concerned about the many areas that didn't have any law and thought there oughta be some way of keepin' the state from becoming a refuge for outlaws. So, he got a few ex-army officers, some former marshals and sheriffs and a few others and formed the Texas Mounted Volunteers. But it's gettin' to be too much for part-time volunteers and I'm thinkin' it'll soon be called somethin' else."

"Sounds interestin'. Are all the outlaws keepin' ya' purty busy?" inquired J.W.

"Oh, it's not too bad. I'm on my way back to San Antone after a little set to I had up past Fort Worth. Seemed a couple fellas got hungry for another man's beef and it didn't set too well with the rancher. So, after we had a bit of discussion with the two fellas, they saw the error of their ways and won't be doin' that again."

"What'd ya have to do?"

"Well, put it this way, the only talkin' that got done was from Mr. Colt."

J.W. reached for his coffee, took a deep swallow and set it down. McGown returned to his plate with a heartiness that could only come from a trail weary and hungry man. Milly convinced J.W. to have another piece of pie and the two men savored the sweetness of the cinnamon and sugar dusted crust over the tasty apple filling. McGown said, "Well, I've got a room above the saloon yonder, how 'bout you?"

"Nah, I'm bunkin' in the livery. That hay mow was too tempting to pass up."

"Well, if you're around for breakfast, we'll see ya then," said McGown as he waved over his shoulder at J.W. Shaking his head, J.W. made his way back to the livery and was soon stretched out in the comfortable hay. He lay for a while with his hands clasped behind his head and staring at the stars through the open hay mow. *What am I gonna do? Flo wanted me to wait here in Waxahachie, but what if her Pa comes lookin' for me? I don't wanna shoot him, cuz if I did, I'd never be able to face Flo. Maybe I could talk to Captain McGown, but I don't want him to know what happened cuz he might wanna take me back, and then what? There's no law in that little place and nothin' to keep McPherson from comin' after me.* He tossed restlessly throughout the night as sleep evaded him. With his mind reliving the events of the past couple days and his fears of the future he fought to clear his mind with prayer. For well over half an hour he sought the face of his God, pleading for some direction or solution to his dilemma. With dawn threatening, he finally fell asleep and snored the early morning hours away.

Chapter Twenty-Four

Dilemma

MILLY GREETED THE LANKY cowboy as he entered the eatery, "Well, mornin' sleepyhead! I thought you cowboys were up 'fore the sun and in the saddle before the crack of dawn." J.W. groaned his howdy and sought a chair at the nearest table. Captain McGown waved him over to his table and greeted him with a "Mornin'," and motioned to Milly to double the order and bring the coffee. The smell of fresh hot coffee brought J.W. a little closer to wakefulness and he eagerly swallowed a big gulp of the steaming hot brew. The captain winced at the thought of such hot liquid burning his mouth but J.W. acted like it didn't bother him at all.

"Looks like you had a rough night, that hay not as comfortable as you thought?" asked the captain.

"Ah, wasn't that. Just got a lot on my mind and couldn't get it stop swirlin' around up there," as he motioned to his tousled hair. His hat joined the hat of the captain on the back of the nearby chair and the two men looked for their breakfast. It was just a short minute before Milly brought the piled high plates and sat them before the men. Huevos Rancheros was the order of the day and the spicy aroma filled the café. The tall stacks of tortillas, red chili sauce, eggs, hash browns and more sauce tempted the men to enthusiastically tackle the mounds.

With their appetite sated, both men leaned back to enjoy some more coffee and a leisurely start to the day. "So, you lookin' for some bad hombres around here are ya'?" asked J.W. of the Captain.

"Nah, just takin' my time gettin' back to San Antone, I don't often get the chance for a comfortable bed and good food so I take advantage of it whenever I can."

J.W. nodded his head and stared at his cup of coffee. He pushed the cup around and back again, fiddled with the spoon and napkin, then spun the cup around again. The Captain recognized when someone had something to talk about and he chose not to push. Letting J.W. take his time, the Captain motioned to Milly for refills. The usually loquacious Milly silently poured the coffee as she looked at the sullen cowboy. With a "Humph" she returned to her kitchen. Finally, J.W. looked up at McGown and said, "I think I need some advice."

"I thought you might have something on your mind. Go ahead, I'm all ears and I'll help if I can," explained the Captain.

J.W. started from the time of his arrival at the ranch and gave the Captain the complete story up to and including the shoot-out at the church. "The last thing I wanted was to shoot him, but I couldn't just stand there and let him shoot me, 'sides, Flo was standin' there beside me and I sure didn't want her to get hit."

The Captain shook his head, spun his own cup and looked up at J.W. and said, "Now I've heard of everything. I never knew of a shootin' at church, boy if that don't beat all," he stated as he shook his head. "But if it happened like you said, and I have no reason to doubt you, then you shouldn't have anything to worry about. It would be a clear cut case of self-defense."

"Well, I figgered it would be, but since there weren't no law down there, I didn't know what to think."

147

"I tell you what. How 'bout you and me goin' back there together and maybe I can get the circuit judge to come with us. It just so happens I had a couple drinks with him last night at the saloon yonder, and I think I can get him to come. But if we all go down there and have a proper trial then when you're exonerated, the Mc . . . what'd you say their name was?"

"McPhersons"

"Yeah, then the McPhersons won't have any reason to be comin' after you. You'll be cleared good and proper. Whatdya say to that?"

J.W. looked up at the Captain, grinned and said, "That would be just fine. It would certainly be a load off my mind and maybe it'd clear things with me and Florence."

"She's the daughter you spoke about, the one you're sweet on?"

"Yeah, we never said as much, but we'd like to be gettin' married and startin' our own family."

Talbot Rollins was the circuit judge for an area bigger than most states. From Fort Worth South to San Antonio, his circuit would usually take two months to cover and with new villages and towns cropping up it could easily take longer. Captain McGown had often brought perpetrators into his court and the two had become friends. Talbot was happy for a break in his routine and gladly acquiesced to McGown's request to change his circuit for a few days and join them on the return trip to the little village that would one day become known as the town of Italy. As they came to the Bell ranch North of town, the Captain asked Josiah, the oldest student from J.W.'s Sunday School, to take word to Florence and the McPhersons that there would be a trial in town at the church house to deal with the shooting at the church. When the trio arrived in the town, word quickly spread of the coming event on the morrow.

The crowd that gathered on that Saturday at the church rivaled the usual crowd for the services on Sunday. The arrangement of the benches and the big desk at the front looked more like the school than the church, but the social gathering didn't preclude the usual conversations and gossip. Sitting on the second row of benches was Florence and her mother, Rebecca McPherson. Notably absent was James Enoch and the brothers. To prevent any discussions, Captain McGown kept J.W. separate from everyone before the trial got underway.

With his personal gavel, the judge said, "Order, order," and as the crowd grew quiet he continued, "I'm Talbot Rollins, circuit judge for the Eighth circuit for the state of Texas and I will preside over this trial. Now we've come together to resolve an incident that happened just a week ago at this very location. Captain J.B. McGown of the Texas Mounted Volunteers has apprised me of the happenings and it is my intention to hear anyone and everyone that holds any information that is pertinent to this event. First, I want to call Pastor Jacob Bell to the stand."

The pastor rose from the crowd and made his way to the front. The judge asked him to stand before him and raise his right hand. The Captain held a Bible before him and asked the pastor to place his left hand on the Bible and listen to the Judge. When he was sworn in, the pastor took a seat on a small bench to the side and the judge began, "Now pastor, would you tell me in your own words what happened on Sunday last?"

The pastor began to recount the events beginning with the dismissal of church services and the beginning of the community meal. As he shared the details of the events, he was very precise in relating the details, position of everyone, dialogue between the men, and the actual shooting and the subsequent departure of J.W. and the events of the rest of the day. The judge commented, "That is a very good description, very detailed, thank you pastor." The judge dismissed Pastor Bell and turned to the crowd. "Now, you have all heard the pastor's account. Is there anyone here that was present at the said event and would have anything to add or anything they think might be different?" As he waited, he looked over the crowd of expectant faces and sought out any raised hands or

149

anything to indicate there was anyone present that might add to the testimony. "Hummm, all right, then if you were present on that day and witnessed what the pastor described, and you agree with everything the pastor said, please raise your hand." Almost the entire crowd raised their hands and those that did not, had not been present at the church last Sunday. The judge continued, "So, those of you with your hands raised believe that this man, J.W. Harpold, acted in self-defense when he shot one Patrick McPherson? If that is so, please keep your hands up." He looked at the crowd and determined there were over forty people that substantiated the pastor's statement. "Very well, I hereby find that J.W. Harpold acted in self-defense on Sunday last when he shot and killed one Patrick McPherson and is hereby exonerated of all charges." He pounded the gavel on the desk to dismiss the proceeding.

The crowd rose to their feet and started making their way to the door. J.W. walked to the waiting Florence and the two embraced with her mother looking on. J.W. turned to Rebecca and said, "Mrs. McPherson, I'm so sorry this had to happen."

"I know, I know, but at least it's over now. And I'm glad James Enoch and the boys weren't here to cause a ruckus. They took the herd down to San Antone to that buyer that was here last week. They won't be back for another week or so. I suggest you not hang around long," she cautioned. J.W. and Florence looked at one another and Florence turned to her mother and said, "Mum, J.W. and I want to get married. We love each other and want to be together." J.W. looked at Florence with a hint of surprise in his expression but his grin showed his agreement.

"I thought as much, and I also thought about how this could play out. Let me suggest something." She sat down on the bench and asked the couple to join her. The church had emptied out and they were alone. Rebecca shared what was on her heart and how she agreed with both J.W. and Florence. "A mother always knows these things, now here's what we'll do . . ." and she shared her plan for the couple.

By mid-afternoon, the women returned to the church. Senora Alvarez had accompanied them and the palomino and a pack horse trailed behind the buckboard. J.W. waited on the steps as they drew the buckboard to a stop. He helped the ladies down, tethered the team and the horses to the hitch rail and joined the women in the church. Pastor Bell and his wife waited for the small group and greeted each one as they approached the front of the church. It was a simple and short ceremony and the couple unashamedly kissed at the conclusion. With congratulations, tears and goodbyes, they were soon on their way to a new life together and away from the only home Flo had ever known.

Chapter Twenty-Five

Discovery

IT WAS A WEARY group of men that rode into the headquarters of the McPherson ranch with horses' heads hanging down and cowboys slouched in their saddles. James Enoch McPherson pushed his men on the return from San Antonio with long days and short nights, but all were happy to be home and were anxious to re-introduce themselves to their bunks. Rebecca McPherson stood near the rail on the veranda and watched as the weary men put up their horses and gear and staggered into the bunk house. James Enoch's pride wouldn't allow him to slouch and he stood straight and tall as he walked to the main house. With saddle bags over his shoulder, his rifle hanging in his hand, the old man gave his welcoming wife a hug and walked into the house. Rebecca followed her husband into the home and took the saddle bags, set them by the door and went to the kitchen to fetch him a cup of fresh hot coffee. He slumped in his chair at the head of the table and welcomed the cup of rejuvenating brew, took a couple of good swallows and set it down. Looking around he asked, "Where the lassie? Sure'n this isn't Sunday, is it?"

Taking a deep breath and sitting down at the table with her husband, Rebecca placed her hand on the big calloused hand of James Enoch and said, "No, it's not Sunday. But Florence is not here. She and J.W. were married and left to start their own home." The tired man's anger flared and fire filled his eyes as he exploded to his feet, spilling the remaining coffee as he jarred the table. "She what?!" he roared hoping he didn't hear right.

"They were married after the trial was over and they've gone to make a home for themselves."

James Enoch began to pace back and forth at the end of the table as he asked, "Trial? What do you mean a trial?"

"J.W. came back with Captain McGown of the Texas Mounted Volunteers and Judge Talbot Chisholm and there was a trial. Everybody was there and the judge listened and he exonerated J.W. with self-defense." James Enoch interrupted with, "But he killed my boy!"

"Patrick was our boy, but you know as well as I do that J.W. acted in self-defense!" she declared.

"First he kills our son, then he steals our daughter! He needs to be stopped, and I'm . . ."

Rebecca stopped him with her hand on her chest and quietly said, "You're not going to do anything! Florence loves that man and I believe he's a good man and he loves her. You will leave them alone and let them live their lives."

He never could win an argument with his wife when she was so calm and quiet. It was a lot easier when he was arguing with a man and they both got loud and angry and could fight it out, but he couldn't fight with Rebecca and she knew it. He grumbled and fussed and fidgeted then declared, "All right woman, I'll heed ye, but I'm telling you and anybody else, if anything happens to that girl I will hunt him down and tear him limb from limb and I'll enjoy doing it! Mark my words!"

Rebecca just nodded at her husband and retreated to the kitchen to help Senora Alvarez prepare the meal. She knew his bluster was his usual attempt to get the last word, but she wouldn't worry about it, her Florence was a strong willed and healthy woman and she and her husband would be fine. She just hoped they wouldn't be too far away so she could visit them and she smiled as she thought about someday becoming a grandmother.

The big smithy smiled as J.W. and Flo reined in their horses at the door of the livery. He greeted them with, "Well, hello again young man. I see you've brought a friend this time, welcome, welcome. I've got room for your horses, but surely you don't want to bed down in the hay mow this time, do you?"

Both J.W. and Flo smiled at his remark and J.W. responded, "Uh, no sir we don't. But we do need to board our horses for a day or so, if that'd be alright?"

"Sure, sure, take your pick, there's lots of stalls open. You know where the oats are," he said as he waved his ever present hammer over his shoulder. The couple stepped down and led the horses into adjoining stalls. J.W. pointed out the bin with the oats to Flo and he began unsaddling the horses and taking a handful of loose hay he gave both mounts and the pack horse a good rub down. With their noses in the grain, neither horse acknowledged the pats on their rumps as the couple shut the stall doors. With bedrolls and saddle bags, they started for the door, stopped and asked the smithy, "Is there a roomin' house in town that might have a room for a couple of nights?"

"Sure, sure, the next street over behind the mercantile, there's a nice white clapboard house that the widow lady, Grace Merrill, rents rooms. It's a nice place."

With a thank you to the smithy, the couple walked to the rooming house, secured a room and freshened up. The pitcher and basin was ample for Flo, but J.W. had to get more water for the layers of dust that clung to his tired frame. Although it wasn't the usual behavior of couples of the time, J.W. and Florence walked the boardwalk side by side and hand in hand. Florence was so happy there was a bounce in her step as she swung their hands back and forth with their pace. J.W. looked down at his bride, smiled and said, "I think I love you, Mrs. Harpold."

"Think? You better know, Mr. Harpold, 'cause if you don't know, we're gonna have to have a serious sit-down talk about this," she stated sternly but mischievously.

"O.K., I know I love you. But what about you, are you still holding a flame for some ol' boyfriend that run out on you?"

"Run out? I'll have you know I never had a boyfriend run out on me, course my brothers did run some off, come to think of it," she snickered but continued, "but the only one I'm holding a flame for is you! And that's because I know I love you!"

The smiling couple stepped into Milly's Eatery and chose a table in the corner. Milly was soon at their side and smiling at J.W. said, "And I thought that sweet talk would never get you a girl and here you are."

"Milly, I'm proud to introduce you to my wife, Florence. Flo, this is the best cook in the county and her apple pies are absolute mouth-watering," he stated as the matronly woman stood with hands on hips.

"And what about my cherry pies?"

"But Milly, you didn't have any cherry pies when I was here last, so I'm just guessing, but I figger they're probably pretty good too."

"Well, if you don't change your tune, you'll never know. It just so happens today is cherry pie day," then looking down at Flo she continued, ". . . so you better get him to sweeten up a little or he won't get any!" Florence giggled as the woman walked away to serve other customers.

"But she didn't ask us what we want," she said as she looked at J.W. with a bewildered expression.

"She only has one thing for each meal, but she'll bring us some and I'm sure it'll be good."

Milly didn't disappoint as she set plates before the couple. Thick sliced pork chops, fried potatoes, corn on the cob and hot refills on their coffee brought smiles to the couple. It had been a long day in the saddle and the aromas that teased the pair magnified their hunger. J.W. started to dig in but was stopped by Florence as she clasped his hand in hers and said, "Don't you want to thank the Lord for our supper?"

Looking at his wife he let a smile paint his face as he replied, "Of course, I guess I was just so hungry I forgot." Bowing his head and squeezing her hand, he prayed for God's blessings and expressed his thanks for not just the meal but for their safety and deliverance and their marriage. With his quiet Amen, he lifted his eyes to his wife's expectant face and said, "Thanks for bein' mine." She smiled and with a bit of a blush, she started her meal.

After their meal, topped off with delicious cherry pie which J.W. declared his favorite, the couple started a leisurely stroll along the boardwalk of the town. Hand in hand they casually walked and looked at the stars and sliver of moon and shared special thoughts. "So, what do we do now?" asked Florence.

"Well, I thought I'd look around tomorrow for any ideas, maybe a job or something, and if nothing shows up, we'd move on to the next place. I'm not sure what the Lord has in store for us, but I'm confident we are here and together because it's His will."

Florence smiled at his reference to 'His will' and said, "I think so too. But what is it you'd like to do, anything special?"

"Well, you know we've talked about this before and we both thought the idea of having our own place where we could have some cattle, raise some crops, maybe some kids, would be great."

"I heard you sneak in that 'maybe some kids'," she smiled up at her man, then continued, "There's something I need to tell you, I was gonna keep it a surprise but I guess it's still a surprise."

"O.K., what do you mean 'a surprise'?"

"Well, before I left the ranch, Mum gave me a package, she said it was my dowry that she and Pa had been setting aside for me. It's enough so that if we find a place, we could outfit it okay or if we need to buy a place, it might help."

J.W. stopped and turned to look at Flo and said, "Really? Wow, that's great! That changes everything, why with what I've got saved, you know from my folks' savings and with what I saved from workin' for your Pa, we should do alright!" He reached down and picked her up and swung her around like a rag doll as she squealed her delight. Setting her down he kissed her with an unexpected tenderness. He smiled down at his bride and said, "Of course you know, this is our honeymoon." She smiled at her husband as he held her around the waist causing her to bend back a little to look into his eyes and said, "Umhumm, I know, so what are we gonna do about it?"

Chapter Twenty-Six

Home

LIKE MOST NEWLYWEDS, the couple were inseparable so when J.W. said he wanted to check the horses, Flo tagged along. They paused to visit with the smithy and after the usual greetings J.W. asked, "Say, by the way, we were thinkin' 'bout settlin' down hereabouts and I was wonderin' if you knew of any places around that might be a good site for a home?"

With a broad smile, the smithy stopped what he was doing and stepped closer to the couple and said, "How 'bout steppin' into my office and let's talk about it," he said as he motioned to an area with a couple ladder back chairs and a stool around a potbellied stove with a coffee pot steaming on top. They seated themselves as the big smithy handed them a couple of enamel coffee cups and poured them a cup of brew that looked so thick it seemed to fall into their cups in chunks, but it was steaming hot and smelled delightful. The smithy seated himself on the stool and with his elbows on his knees, he held his cup before him. "Now, first off, my name is Sven Jorgensen and you are . . .?"

"Oh, I'm sorry, I plumb forgot. I'm J.W. Harpold and this is my wife, Florence," he shared as he reached forth his hand to shake. Sven gladly shook hands and nodded his head to Flo with a "Ma'am."

"So, what are you two young people looking for when you said 'a place'?"

"Well, we don't rightly know, but I reckon we'll know it when we see it. You know, we'd like a piece of land that would be big enough to get a start on some crops, maybe a few head of cows and such, just a place we can call home and make a livin' on."

"Ah, I see. Well, since you came in yesterday, I was thinkin' you might be needin' a place with your new bride and all," nodding to Flo, ". . . and I think I know a place that would suit."

"Really?" interrupted J.W. excitedly, "Tell us about it."

Sven chuckled at the young man's excitement that was echoed in the face of his wife and began, "A couple years back there was a couple like you that started a place over West of here. They built a cabin and a barn and started out pretty good, but the wife got homesick for her family back East and just couldn't take it out here. Then when the Comanche had a few raids in the area and their neighbors were killed, that was more than she could stand. When they finally decided to give up, they didn't have much, so they traded me the place for a team and a wagon so they could go back home. Now, I haven't even been out to the place in over a year and it's all growed up with weeds and such, needs a lot of work and I don't need it and for that matter, don't even want it. So, if you like it and want it and will put some work into it, I'll let you have if for . . . oh, let's say, half of the first crop you bring in," he said with a broad grin on his grease smeared face.

The couple sat completely still, mesmerized by the offer of the big smithy, and as smiles started to stretch to dimples, they looked at each other and nodded their heads in agreement. Turning to Sven, J.W. asked, "Can we go take a look at it?"

"Sure, sure," and standing and stepping to the open door he pointed to the West and continued, ". . .just take that road yonder, it goes West a spell, then turns North. After about three miles and a wide curve to the left, you'll see an old roadway that forks off between two posts, if they're still there, and winds back along a small creek to the cabin and the barn. They ain't much, but with a little work, they'll be a start for you."

The excited couple started to the stalls for their horses and J.W. said to Flo, "How bout you goin' to Milly's and have her fix us up sumpin' for our noonin' and I'll saddle the horses and pick you up there."

"Okay, hurry though, I'm anxious to see what might be our new home!" she declared as she quickly left the livery.

Leading the two horses, J.W. walked the short distance to Milly's arriving just as Flo exited with a bundle held out before her and smiling in anticipation. A quick stop at the rooming house for their saddle bags, rifle and bedrolls, the two anxious newlyweds were on their way. The three miles were covered in just a short while and the place was easily found with the directions supplied. Riding up to the cabin, they stepped down and tethered their mounts at the corner of the cabin to a cedar post with a metal ring. The log cabin was built solidly from hardwoods that apparently came from by the nearby creek. The chinking was falling out and in places there was none. The steps to the porch were flat rocks and the porch planks were sagging but the roof appeared to still be in good shape. The plank door hung ajar on dried leather hinges and they pushed it aside to step into the cabin. Spider webs blocked their way but J.W. pushed them aside only to step into some sort of nest that a varmint left behind. As they walked in and brushed at more cobwebs, Flo walked to the fireplace and grabbed the swinging metal arm used for hanging pots and pulled it out a bit accompanied by a loud squeal from the slightly rusted metal. There was a table that teetered on three legs and three overturned chairs that cluttered the room, but a sturdy counter and shelving appeared undamaged. There was a window with one shattered pane and three too dirty to see through and shutters that hung on leather hinges. The plank floor, which was unusual for a farm house of the era, was solid but held a considerable amount of debris. The leftovers from visiting animals included a few small bones and bits of fur. Pushing open the door to another room, the light from the window showed a spacious room that apparently served as a bedroom.

"I like it!" declared Flo, "I think it'll be real nice after we get it cleaned up and fixed up a little. You know, some curtains there," pointing to the window," and a solid table and chairs. You know, the stuff that makes a home!"

J.W. smiled at his wife and chuckled, "I'm sure you could make just about any place into a home Flo, I don't have any doubt about that. But you're right, I think it could be a pretty nice place. "Then with an arm around her waist he said, "Let's go take a look at the barn."

Stepping through and around the random weeds, the couple made their way to the barn, entered and looked around. There were three stalls on one side, a large stall on the other and the rest was open without any dividers. A couple of shelves hung on an outside wall while a couple of makeshift saddle racks extended from the wall by the front door. The front door to the barn hung from rollers suspended on a long metal rail and easily slid from side to side. Overall it was in better shape than the house. The back door to the barn led to a large corral with a hay bunker along one side and solid posts and pole rails that showed no sign of weakness. J.W. said, "This looks good, I think it'll do nicely. There's room for all three horses, a good loft for any hay we might be able to bring in, and even room for a milk cow, if we want one. Yeah, I like it!" he declared to the satisfaction of his wife.

Two large elm tree spread shade across the yard to the side of the house and the couple found an area with few weeds and some green grass to spread their blanket and ready their noon meal. Florence was humming a tune as she joyfully laid out the wrapped sandwiches and other treats provided by Milly, while J.W. leaned against the tree watching his wife and thinking about how lucky he was to have such a woman for his wife. He smiled as she looked up at him and asked, "What?"

"Oh nothing, I was just thinking how lucky I am to have you and how God has already blessed us with a home. I think it's going to be a fine place, don't you?" he asked as he looked around at the countryside.

"Yes, I do, and as soon as we eat, I think we should go back to town and get the things we're going to need and get started," she said resolutely.

The ride back to town was filled with ideas, plans, hopes and wishes as the couple chattered on about their new home. Children on Christmas morning couldn't have been happier or more excited than the Harpolds. Their first stop was at the livery to thank Sven and let him know they definitely wanted the place and after shaking hands on the deal, Sven said he'd get the necessary papers ready and would come out to visit them. They rented a buckboard for their supplies, put the pack horse in the harness, settled up for the boarding of the horses and the buckboard and went to the mercantile to start their shopping. Their shopping list grew as they found things that they would need to start their dream that hadn't been on the original list. With the pile of supplies and gear growing, the merchant began to wonder if this new couple would be able to pay for it all. But to his surprise and delight, J.W. readily settled up their bill and started loading the buckboard. With a broom, shovels, carpentry tools, bedding, ticking, powder and lead, and on and on, the pile grew but was manageable for the buckboard. Tying their horses to the back of the wagon, they headed out to their new home. It was late in the afternoon and they had a lot of work before them, but they were excited about their new home.

The dust cloud raised by her enthusiastic sweeping caused Flo to cough and sneeze and run outside to get some fresh air. Bending over and slapping at her skirt to rid it of the excess dust, she coughed again and waved her hand in front of her face to dispel the cloud of dust. J.W. stood in the doorway of the barn looking at his wife in the reflected glow of the sunset and smiled at his beauty, then hollered, "Hey, what're you tryin' to do, start a tornado?"

With another cough, she straightened up and laughed and said, "I don't need to start it, it's already goin' inside!" she declared as she pointed to the door. Returning to the doorway to the bedroom, she grabbed the shovel leaning by the door and placing it on the floor, swept the pile of dirt into it, took it to the front door and threw it out right into the middle of her husband. He jumped back as she put her hand to her mouth and started laughing. "Now, you're just as dirty as I am, ain't we a pair!"

Working together, the cobwebs were soon gone and the dirt and dust evacuated sufficiently for them to roll out their blankets on the floor of the bedroom. But before she would turn in for the night, Florence said, "We need to get rid of this dust," motioning to her front," . . . and we need water for coffee in the morning. So, how 'bout you carrying the bucket and I'll carry the lantern and we'll make a trip to the creek to take care of that, O.K.?" Although the dirt didn't bother J.W. as much as it did Flo, he readily agreed and the jaunt to the creek was made under the clear canopy of stars and a sliver of moon. It was a pleasant night for a swim in the small creek and they appreciated the dug-out pool provided by the previous owners, the Millers. It was a great end to the first day in their new home, and they both knew there would be many more nights like this before them.

Chapter Twenty-Seven

Settling

Well over a year had passed with just two letters from her daughter and Rebecca McPherson was getting anxious to see the girl. She was determined she would not let another year pass without visiting the couple and she had formulated a plan for that to happen. Now it was just a matter of getting her husband to understand and allow her to make the trip. Tonight at supper was the designated time in her mind and she was committed. With Senora Alvarez preparing James Enoch's favorite meal of buffalo hump roast, fresh dug potatoes with gravy, corn on the cob and a wilted lettuce salad, she knew her husband would be in as close to an agreeable mood as was possible for the stubborn Scotsman.

Leaning back in his chair and patting his belly, the big Scotsman said, "Woman, that was a mighty fine meal," then turning toward the kitchen he raised his voice, ". . . and Senora Alvarez, you done mighty fine, thank you." But the man knew much of the work had been done by his wife and thought she might be up to something so he prepared himself as he looked to his mate. "So, what is it, why am I being spoiled like this?"

Rebecca leaned her elbows on the table at looked directly at her man and stated rather than asking, "I'm going to visit our daughter. Sean will drive me in our new buggy and we'll be safe enough. It's only two days to where they are and I should be back in just over a week."

"Oh is that so? And what if I don't think you ought to go?" he said leaning on the table.

Scooting a little closer to him she said with a smile and a calm voice, "I will listen to you but I'm going anyway." Smiling, she tucked her hand under her chin and blinked her lashes at him.

He took a deep breath that raised his shoulders, let it out and said as grumpily as he could muster, "Oh, all right. I 'spose you can go, but don't you stay longer than you said. You're pretty important around here, y'know." Rebecca knew that was as close as he could come to saying he would miss her and she smiled at her big tough red bearded Scotsman, stood up and leaned over to plant a kiss on the narrow lips that hid in the mass of red whiskers.

"Thank you dear," she said as she swished her way to their bedroom.

Florence stood on tiptoes on the porch to look as far down the road as she could see, trying to determine if the buggy coming up the road was anyone she knew. J.W left with the sunrise for a short hunting trip to resupply their meat-stores, and she was slightly apprehensive as to who might be visiting. She didn't think any of her neighbors had a buggy like that one, it had two seats and a fringed top and was pulled by a matched pair of blacks. *What a grand buggy, but who could it be?* she thought as she considered getting her pistol from the cabin. A waving hanky from the passenger caught her attention and then she recognized who was visiting. Her mother and her brother! She jumped up and down and clapped her hands with her excitement and watched the buggy pull up to the cabin with two people grinning broadly. Florence squealed like a young girl as the buggy stopped and Sean started down to help his mother. He was met by a rousing hug from his sister and as soon as she released him, he reached to assist his mother as she stepped down. The two women hugged, squeezed, patted and squealed together with the delight of the reunion.

Flo quickly ushered her mother into the cabin and shooed her brother to the barn to put up the horses. Rebecca seated herself at the table as Flo filled the coffee pot to heat some water for tea. Flo's mother never acquired the taste for coffee like her husband did and preferred tea, the only hot drink allowed in her home as she was growing to adulthood. Although Florence preferred coffee, she always enjoyed a leisurely cup of tea with her mother. This was a routine greatly missed and she now took great care to properly prepare the tea for her Mum. The water was heating on the stove as she prepared the ceramic tea pot, the ball of tea and the new tea cozy, just presented to her by her mother. When the coffee pot started rocking a little on the hot stove, she grabbed it up, put a little in the tea pot to rinse it and pre-heat it, then filled the tea pot and dropped in the tea ball. Securing the lid on the pot, she placed the knitted tea cozy on the pot to keep the heat in as the tea steeped.

Seating herself at the table, she stretched forth her hands to take her mother's hands and looked Rebecca in the eye as she said, "I can't wait another minute! I'm so glad you're here and I can see your face when I tell you!"

"Tell me what?" asked Rebecca with a sober and concerned look on her face.

Flo's face glowed with excitement and the grin that split her face foretold something good. She shrugged her shoulders and squeezed her mother's hands as she said, "You're going to be a grandmother!" Rebecca's expression immediately changed to one of joy and happiness as she gripped her daughter's hands a little tighter and her eyes welled up with water as she forced a smile at her daughter. Then she let the tears fall, "Oh, I'm so happy for you!" then leaning toward her only girl, she continued, ". . . when is it due? I'll have to come back!"

"In the Spring, I think, and yes you will have to come back!"

And the chattering began and her brother leaned against the pillar of the porch, shook his head and chuckled as he thought *They sound like a whole passel of chipmunks fighting over a couple of nuts!* Looking up at a movement caught out of the corner of his eye, Sean spotted J.W. walking his horse from the trees by the creek with the deer carcass across the rump of his mount. With the buggy and team in the barn, the only evidence of visitors was the shadowy figure on the porch and J.W. pulled up to get a better look. There shouldn't be anybody around except Flo and the figure on the porch sure wasn't wearing a dress. He kneed his horse slowly forward and the figure stepped from the porch to the stone and the brightness from the setting sun revealed a familiar figure. Sean waved at the distant figure of J.W. and started to walk to the barn to intercept his brother-in-law.

The two men met at the barn door and Sean smiled up at J.W. who sat easy but with a stern expression not knowing what to think. *Is the old man here, and is he gonna cause trouble?* he thought. Rebecca had written Florence and explained the vow made by the old man and J.W. thought caution was needed as he extended his hand to Sean. "Howdy. Who all's with you?"

Sean immediately picked up on J.W.'s apprehension and said, "Just me and Mum, Pa's not here."

J.W. relaxed and stepped down from his big grey, drug the carcass off and started putting up his horse. "So, how is everybody?" asked J.W. to start their conversation.

"Oh, everybody's fine. Mum was just missing Flo and had to come check on her little girl."

"Yeah, Flo was feeling the same and had been talking about making a trip down to see her folks. It's good that you came, Flo will certainly be happy about it." The men continued a casual conversation typical of two men and that amounted to no more than a couple dozen words. Men just don't have the same need as women when it comes to hearing themselves talk and carrying on conversations and the two brothers-in-law had never been close. They walked back to the cabin and as they entered, the women came to their feet to greet them. Putting his floppy felt hat on the peg by the door, J.W. turned to catch his wife as she jumped up to give him a welcome home kiss. Leaning closely, she whispered to J.W., "I told Mum, but Sean doesn't know, you can tell him." J.W. just responded with a smile, a nod of his head and a muttered, "Uhmmhumm."

The next two days were spent with the women either in the house at the table or strolling around the place arm in arm, but it seemed they didn't pause long enough in their visiting to hardly take a breath. J.W. enjoyed showing Sean around and the younger brother showed genuine interest in what the couple had accomplished. With pride, J.W. said, "You shoulda seen that roof," as he pointed to the cabin, "I thought I would fall through, some of the holes were so big. But fortunately there was a good straight cedar up on the bluff that made good shingles. And that chinking, it took a while to get it right, 'cause I never thought about using salt but the neighbor gave me the mix and it's done a good job. "

"I can tell you're really enjoyin' havin' your own place. From what Flo told us, you both have been pretty busy fixin' up and stuff, and the place looks good. Real homey, ya' know?" observed Sean. The developing friendship between the two men showed J.W. was pleased to hear the comment from his brother-in-law.

"Thanks, it's been rewarding. When we first saw the place, well, we didn't hardly, cuz the weeds were so thick and tall. Now we've got two fields with crops comin' on, and a good sized pasture over there for the cows, even though we've only got a dozen. It is making into a pretty good place. I never thought I'd have a place like this, but it's home now."

"Uh, there's somethin' else I need to say," started Sean, and with a short pause he continued, "all that stuff with Pa, you know, 'bout him threatenin' you, I'm not part of that. What you did you couldn't help and Patrick pushed it and I don't hold that against you, alright?"

J.W. extended his hand to shake Sean's as he smiled and replied, "That's good to hear, thanks!"

J.W. didn't want to dwell on the uncomfortable topic and pointed out the garden spot that Flo had insisted on and was now in full growth. He commented, "Sometimes I think she likes that garden more'n me, she spends more time with the garden, that's for sure. But I guess it's payin' off, we've been eating pretty good out of it."

J.W. and Flo stood side by side and waved at the retreating buggy. Her mother was turned around in the seat and busily waving a hanky in the air as her goodbye. Flo dabbed at a tear and asked, "What'd Sean say when you told him?"

With a bewildered frown he asked, "Told him what?"

She elbowed him in the ribs and said, "J.W. Harpold, you had better tell me you told him or I'm gonna hit you again!"

"I didn't tell him; men don't talk about those things like you women do."

She looked at the disappearing buggy and began to smile, "Momma's gonna be wonderin' what to talk about all the way home until she finds out he doesn't know, then he'll be filled to overflowing with Momma's braggin' about the baby!" She giggled as J.W. held her tight beside him. He looked down at her upturned smile and lifted her to her tiptoes to plant a kiss.

Chapter Twenty-Eight

Neighbors

THE DEDICATION OF THE NEW building for St. Mary's Catholic Church was a community wide affair. The other church in town, Community Baptist, in an effort to show mutual commitment and support, encouraged their congregation to attend the dedication at St. Mary's and wish their neighbors well. It was a grand time for all that were in attendance, the rituals and liturgy of the Catholics were very impressive and somber with the recited prayers, the tinkling of the bells and the beautiful trappings of the altar and the priests as well. The priest was addressed as Father Sullivan and his attendants, several boys in black and white outfits, followed him throughout the ceremony. J.W. was spellbound with all the ritual having never attended a church like this before and like most of the visitors, he didn't know what to say or do and just watched the crowd to follow suit. After all the prayers, standing and sitting and bowing and kneeling, J.W. was a little exasperated but still very impressed. As the crowd filed out of the building, the priest was standing by the door and greeting and thanking everyone that attended. Following his wife with the crowd, J.W. reached the door and when the priest extended his hand J.W. gave a firm handshake and said, "Well sir, you sure have a fine building here and all those crosses, drapes, and candles and everything, it sure is pretty."

"Well thank you sir," replied the priest and continued, ". . . thank you for coming and feel free to come back anytime."

J.W. just nodded his head and followed his wife and the rest of the crowd down the steps. Looking around he said to Flo, "I guess they don't know how to eat as good as the Baptists. Can you believe it, not a thing to eat anywhere!"

Flo just giggled at her big hungry man and said, "Is that all you think of, something to eat. That's not what church is for, you're supposed to be thinking about other things, don'tcha know?"

"I was, I was thinkin' about beef and pork and chicken and salad and…"

Flo poked him in the ribs, put her hand through his arm and said, "Oh, all right. Let's go home and I'll fix you something to eat, you big lummox you." Her laughter was contagious and J.W. joined her in the levity. "Well, a growin' boy has to eat ya know," he declared. Rubbing her tummy with the slight swell, she answered, "Yes, a growing boy has to eat."

The couple recently became the proud owners of a new buckboard, or at least it was new to them, and now made their way to the wagon and team. As he was helping Flo into the seat, he heard a hail from behind him he turned to see their neighbors, the Brooke's. Peter and Sally and their two-year-old son, Elijah, had been their closest neighbor for the past six months. The couple moved into the old Gilbertson place and had been faced with about the same amount of work that J.W. and Florence did when they arrived. The two couples actually met at church and were pleased to find out they were neighbors. Many was the time when the couples helped each other with the larger projects of building, or rather re-building, their homes.

"Hey neighbor! So, J.W., are you thinkin' what I'm thinkin' since the good Catholics don't understand the Baptist tradition of having lots of dinners?"

"If you mean am I thinkin' about food, yes I am. I'm so hungry my belly button's pinchin' my backbone!"

"That ain't nuthin', during the ceremony in there my wife jumped and started to lookin' around for a bear she thought got in the church, but it was just my stomach growlin' fer attention!"

The women laughed together and nodding their heads in agreement, they leaned toward one another and chatted quietly with their plans, while the men continued to lie to each other trying to outdo one another. After a big belly laugh erupted from the two, their wives said simply, "We can go now," and motioned for the men to get a move on, and the chuckling friends slapped the reins to their teams to trot down the road towards home. The Brooke's place was just across the creek bottom and the two houses were visible to one another with the Brooke's home build on the shoulder of a slight rise beyond the tree-line of the creek. There was a nice clearing in the trees by the creek-side that had become a joint picnic spot for the two families and once again it would be the site of a neighborly visit between the couples.

They had an enjoyable afternoon together as the ladies chattered on about babies and families while the men talked crops, farm-work, and hunting. This would probably be the last time for a picnic this season with the fall colors starting to paint the groves of trees along the creek bottom. The men discussed the need to stock up their meat larder and agreed that a day of hunting would be necessary so they planned for the hunt on the morrow. With the sun dancing on the treetops and the cool of the coming evening making itself known, the good friends parted company and with hands full of baskets and blankets made their way home.

"I always enjoy visiting with Sally, even though I hardly get a word in edgewise, she's just so bubbly and girly all the time. And we have so much in common, she's actually from a Scottish background also, did you know that?" she asked her husband.

"Uh, what'd ya say? I'm sorry, I was thinkin' about our huntin' trip in the mornin' and I didn't hear what you said," answered J.W. apologetically.

"Oh, that's all right, I know you and Peter are takin' off in the mornin' to do your manly thing of hunting," and as J.W. started to protest, she continued, "Oh, I know we need the meat and I'm not depriving you men of your hunting trip. Sally and I might get together tomorrow just to visit some more, too."

They walked together arm in arm back up the slight slope to their cabin and enjoyed every step together. With their minds traveling in different directions but their feet following the same path, they dropped into the suspended swing on their porch. As the half-moon was rising before the sun had set, the clear sky promised a fair weather day for their planned adventures of tomorrow.

The hunt that started with the sunrise had yielded no game as mid-day approached. The men followed the creek bottom upstream and were now over ten miles from home. J.W. put up his hand as they cleared the trees, he thought he heard something and cocked his head in an attempt to identify the sound. He looked at a ravine that came from an escarpment at the crest of a small mesa and just beyond the ridge he saw a slight cloud of dust. Then he heard it again, a bellow from a bull buffalo. He looked quickly at Peter and motioned for him to grab his rifle and follow. Approaching the ridge on foot, the two men hunkered down and continued their climb up the ridge. As they neared the top, they bellied down and crawled to the crest. As they looked over they were surprised to see a small herd of about fifteen buffalo with two young bulls sparring on the far side. The dust they had seen was from the two bulls pawing at the dirt and throwing the dust over their humps. The herd was between eighty and one hundred yards from the men. J.W. turned to Peter and said, "We only need one apiece, so pick a good cow that doesn't have a calf at her side and when you're ready, let me know."

"I ain't never shot a buffalo before, anything I should know?" asked Peter.

"Nah, I think your Hawken will put it down O.K., just don't try no head shot, their skulls are too thick! Take it in the heart, you know, right behind their front leg down low."

Looking the animals over, Peter settled on his target, identified it to J.W. and was told, "O.K. whenever you're ready, go 'head on. I'm takin' that cow that's watchin' the bulls. I think she's lovesick enough to not be in a hurry to move."

Peter chuckled a bit and said, "All right, here goes." He squeezed off his shot and J.W.'s shot was so close behind, the thunder of the combined reports caused the entire herd to jump as if they were on ground that moved. As the smoke cleared, the remaining herd trotted away leaving the two carcasses behind. When Peter saw his animal down he said, "Whoopee, I got it! Now we're gonna have some good eatin'."

"Yeah, but now the fun's over and the work begins," proclaimed his hunting partner.

Mid-morning and Florence was on her knees in her garden pulling weeds and harvesting the mature crops. She was in a pair of men's britches held up by suspenders and rolled up at her ankles, it was much easier weeding the garden with britches than a big skirt, besides she had to save her dresses for more important days. She leaned back on her heels, used the back of her hand to push her hair away from her sweating brow and took a deep breath as she proudly surveyed her garden. Remembering the day before and the time spent with the Brooke's, Florence glanced toward her friend's house on the distant rise. She gasped as she saw a tendril of smoke rising from the far side of the house. Standing to her feet to get a better look, she shaded her eyes and unconsciously leaned slightly forward. Afraid of what she was seeing, she dropped her trowel and ran to the barn. She opened the stall of her palomino, Blondie, hastily put the bridle on and with a couple of steps and a hop she swung aboard the bare backed mare, seated herself and grabbing a handful of mane, she dug her heels into the palomino's ribs and they left the barn at a full run. Leaning down on her horse's neck, she spoke to her four-legged friend saying, "Come on girl, we gotta get there in a hurry!" *Oh, I hope she's all right, please Lord, keep Sally and Elijah safe* she prayed as she rode. Stealing a glance in the direction of the neighbor's house, her heart leaped as she saw the column of smoke thickening and spreading a thick black and grey cloud of doom.

As the palomino stretched out and climbed the slight rise, Flo frantically searched the area for any sign of Sally and Elijah. None. No movement anywhere, though she heard alarmed animals whinnying and bawling from the barn, there was no sign of her friend. She pulled Blondie to a sliding stop before the cabin and screamed, "Sally! Sally! Where are you Sally!" She fanned the smoke from her face, bent down to see below the spreading cloud and saw the door was slightly ajar. Without thinking, just reacting, she ran to the door and hollered into the smoke filled room, "Sally! Sally! Where are you Sally?" Pulling out her shirttail and putting it to her mouth and nose, she started into the smoke filled cabin. Within just a couple of steps, she saw some material moving on the floor. Dropping to her knees to see beneath the smoke, she saw her friend on the floor clutching her son. They apparently tried to get out and were overcome by the smoke. Flo quickly reached out and grabbing her friend under her arm pits she leaned back and started to drag them out. She stumbled backwards and fell, catching herself but starting a coughing fit. She stretched out on her stomach toward the open door, sucked in lungs full of air, turned and grabbed her friend again. She could see the flames climbing the walls at the far side of the house next to the fireplace. With a new dose of determination, she leaned back, took another step, leaned back and repeated it over and over until she finally was through the door. Even though semiconscious, Sally had tenaciously held on to her son and Florence finally had them off the stoop and onto the ground. It was easier dragging them on the gravelly dirt path, but her strength began to wane. She dropped to her knees and with shoulders heaving fought to gain more air. Finally, after several moments that seemed like years, Flo fell back, sat up and pulled her friends head to her lap and prayed, *Lord please, bring her back, her family needs her, oh please God help her.*

A cough from the prone figure on her lap startled Flo but as Sally continued to cough, Flo turned her attention to the boy. He was limp, but he was breathing and with Sally coming around, the two women focused on the boy and rolled him to his stomach and thumped on his back to try to get him to clear his lungs. Soon all three were coughing, laughing and crying together with tears leaving trails down smoke blackened cheeks. Then looking at each other, the two women smiled and hugged tightly and their friendship took on another level of commitment and appreciation.

There was nothing they could do for the house; the fire had grown beyond their ability to fight it. They were just thankful that no life was lost. As they watched the roof fall in and the walls lean toward each other, the women grasped hands and let the tears slide unhindered. When the last wall fell amidst a cloud of smoke and flying embers, the women heard the clatter of hooves and the sound of trace chains. They turned to see two wagons full of people coming from the town and other nearby neighbors to offer their help. The women stood to greet them, waved them over to the trees where they stood and as many of the women stepped down to comfort them, the men started closer to the fire and with hands in pockets, they watched the rest of the timbers be consumed by the remaining flames. As the fire died down, the many visitors expressed their sorrow to Sally and promised to return to help with the re-build. Some of the women offered to bring some clothes and other necessities and were told to bring them to the Harpold's as the Brooke's would be staying with them for the

176

next few days. With Elijah astraddle the palomino, the two
women walked hand in hand back to the cabin of J.W. and Flo.

Chapter Twenty-Nine

Amy

THAT FALL EVERY spare moment was spent helping the Brooke's rebuild their home. Between the two men, a solution was found to every problem that arose from their inexperience but their enthusiasm and determination always found a way, maybe not always the right way, but a way nevertheless. Florence started calling J.W. her walking shadow because of always coming home covered head to toe with soot from the charcoal and ash. But when they completed the new cabin, it was bigger and better than what they had before. Also built out of logs using J.W.'s formula for chinking of clay, salt and ashes, they had a solid and tight new home.   The church community had rallied and provided clothing and household goods and other supplies that were destroyed in the inferno. The Brooke's expressed their appreciation to all the members of the community and their church that had given so much help. The sharing of their travail and the answers to prayer brought tears to everyone present and culminated in an old fashioned hug fest.

The winter was a mild one with only enough snow to turn the ground white on two occasions. But central Texas was not known for severe or even difficult winters and as the Bluebonnets started pushing their way toward the spring sun, longer warmer days were the norm. Flo's mother, Rebecca was already on her way to her daughter's for the anticipated arrival of her first grandchild. A very uncomfortable Flo stood on her porch waving at the arriving buggy driven by her brother Sean and carrying an excited Rebecca and another woman unknown to Flo. No sooner had Rebecca touched ground and she was introducing the visitor. "Flo, this is your Aunt Ida! You remember her, course you were just a little thing the last time she visited, but maybe you do remember?"

"Uh, no, but I do remember you talking about a younger sister named Ida, is this the same sister?" asked Flo.

"Of course dear, she recently moved to Waxahachie. Her husband, Thurgood, is the new manager of the bank in town and she's going to be your neighbor as well as your aunt. Isn't that lovely?"

The animated greetings between mother and daughter and aunt filled the little cabin with squeals and laughter and soon became a steady stream of conversation. Flo was full of questions about her pregnancy and the coming birth and Rebecca was thrilled with the opportunity to share her experiences and knowledge with her beautiful daughter. J.W. was busy plowing and planting and tending to his growing herd of cattle, now numbering fifteen. When the sweaty, smelly, tired husband arrived at the cabin, he was greeted by his brother-in-law Sean with a friendly handshake and a barrage of questions about his place and work. J.W. was pleased to share the details of their winter past and continued answering questions while he stripped to the waist and cleaned up at the washstand beside the house. With the family gathered around the only table, the conversation flowed and a fine dinner was enjoyed. The coming event of the birth of the first child was unpredictable at best, but Rebecca planned on staying with the

Harpold's no matter how long the wait for her first grandchild. Sean took Aunt Ida back to town and returned to his bunk in the barn.

The next ten days were monotonous in the routine of spring farm work. Fields prepared and seeded, garden plot spaded and planted, and J.W. did a little extra as he planted rose bushes near the house as a special favor for his treasured wife. Wednesday was an uncomfortable day for the expectant mother, but Thursday started with discomfort, pains, and the unmistakable indication of a coming baby with the breaking of her water. The neighbors had already decided on an alarm signal and J.W. ran outside and set a torch under the prepared small bonfire that was covered with green branches that would send up a pillar of white smoke. With the fire started, J.W. ran back inside and offered to help only to be told by his mother-in-law, "Oh, why don't you go plow something or other. We'll let you know when you can come back in, now shoo, shoo!" J.W. almost knocked Sally over as she was rushing into the house, but stepping aside to let the exiled husband pass, she soon joined the women with the 'birthing business.'

Amy Etelka Harpold bounced into the world with a good shock of hair, dimples on her cheeks and her knees, and a smile that stretched from father to mother. The new parents were busting with pride as grandmother Rebecca handed the baby to the new father. Afraid he would break something, he was hesitant to turn back the blanket with his calloused hands, but couldn't resist looking at the perfect little baby. Surely she was the most beautiful baby ever born and if you don't believe it all you had to do was ask J.W. The bedroom was full with Grandmother Rebecca, Aunt Ida, neighbor Sally and her son, Elijah who couldn't understand what all the fuss was about, and father J.W. He lay the baby in her mother's arms and reached for his wife's hand. He looked around the room and asked, "Can we pray?" and continued, "Dear Heavenly Father, we are so thankful to you for this gift of new life and for the care you've shown to this family. We ask you to keep your hands

180

on the baby and the new mother as they walk together into this new life set before us. God, give me the wisdom and strength to be the man, father, and husband that your Word sets the standards for and that we will be the family that you require. Thank you Father. We pray in Jesus' name, Amen." The stillness of the room was soon dispelled with the first feeble cries of the newborn. While Rebecca helped Florence, the others left the room and gathered on the porch. Congratulations were shared among the growing group of concerned neighbors, friends and church family. Little Amy was the first newborn for the community this year and everyone wanted to share in the celebration. With the many dishes brought by others, it was easy to assemble an impromptu pot-luck supper that was ample for everyone present.

Rebecca stayed for another week and J.W. was glad for the extra helping hand from Sean. By the time Grandmother Rebecca was ready to leave, the crops were all planted, the garden was set and the rose bushes were thriving. With spring painting the fields and hillsides with a variety of greens and bright colors of early blossoms, Rebecca and Florence hugged one another and with tears on her cheeks and a babe in her arms, Florence waved good bye to her mother and her brother as the buggy disappeared down the lane.

The new baby girl was a magnet for curious women that made a steady stream of visitors to the Harpold cabin. Every one that came also brought either a prepared dish of food or the makings for a meal, all to help the busy new mom and the changing routine of the household. Aunt Ida was a frequent visitor and Sally couldn't stay away and was and welcome and constant attending nurse as she spent so much time with her friend and the new baby. Elijah had become a protective big brother and was often found looking into the basinet at the happy baby.

J.W. sat spread legged on the floor and Florence was in a similar position about eight feet away. Flo held both hands of the toddling little girl, now well past her first birthday, and looked at J.W. as she spoke to the child, "Go ahead, go to Daddy," as she leaned forward with the first tentative step, then another and as J.W. reached for her hands, she took another and one step totally free before being caught by her waiting father. Both parents laughed and smiled at each other and their precious Amy. Turning her around, the exercise was repeated with all the baby talk encouragement and claps and cheers. But hearing the sounds of an approaching wagon, Flo looked at J.W. and asked, "Is that a wagon coming?" J.W. stood and went to the door to investigate. Stepping outside to the porch, he saw the familiar buggy from the McPhersons coming up the road. He hollered back over his shoulder, "I think it's your mother!" Flo jumped up with the girl in her arms and went to the door in time to see the buggy pull to a stop in front of the house. The fragrance of full blossomed roses caught her attention and she looked down at the bushes that were almost as tall as the railing on the porch. The front of her home was almost a blanket of red roses from side to side and the fragrance was wonderful.

She looked back at the buggy and was surprised to see only Sean and watched as he stepped down. With a somber face he wasted no time as he said, "It's Mum, she's wasting away and has been asking for you. Can you come?"

"Of course, but what's wrong with her? Has she had a doctor or anybody?" the confusion and concern flooded her with questions she couldn't utter because of a throat constricted with fear. As Sean followed her back into the cabin, he started explaining how their mother had been failing for a few months. When they were finally able to get someone to come see her, it was a doctor that was also a drunk, but he was known as an able physician when he was sober. They caught him on a good day and his visit to the bedside of their mother resulted in a diagnosis of consumption. What would later be known as tuberculosis, consumption was kind of a catch-all diagnosis for many illnesses that were unknown or undetectable in the time. With consumption thought to be contagious, Flo was concerned about the baby and insisted J.W. accompany them and take care of the baby while she visited her mother. Then remembering her Aunt Ida, she said, "We better let Aunt Ida know, she might want to come with us." The two women had grown closer in these last few months. Ida was several years younger than her sister Rebecca and with so little age difference, had become a good friend to Flo.

It would be a difficult trip and Flo needed her husband by her side, regardless of the potential conflict with her father. J.W. knew it might be an anxious time but also knew Flo must be with her mother and he wouldn't ask her to face that alone. It would be a two-day trip and they began immediately with preparations to leave with the sunup.

Chapter Thirty

Passing

IT WAS A FRAIL FIGURE of a woman that welcomed Flo and Ida with a weakly raised hand and a forced smile. With eyes sunken deep into dark sockets, thin wisps of hair that drooped over wrinkled ears, skeletal arms that struggled to lift bony fingers, and a thin frame that was not hidden under the wispy night gown, Rebecca struggled to give a welcome smile. Propped on two pillows and fighting for breath, Rebecca was glad to see her daughter and sister but knew her appearance would be startling to the two women. Upon entering the room and at first glance of her mother, Florence rushed to the bedside and knelt with her hands outreached to touch the delicate hands of her mother. Ida ran to join Flo at the side of her sister. The two visitors were at a loss for words and Florence could only say, "Oh mother . . . " as she bent to kiss the back of her mother's hand. Ida turned her head away and daubed at the tears that blurred her vision. Their helplessness compounded the mix of emotions that fought within their minds and hearts as Rebecca forced a weak smile and in a whisper said, "I'm so

glad you came, I was afraid . . ." and turned her head away to
hide the tears.

"Oh mother, I wish I'd known sooner. I'd have been here
with you," the words came from a distraught face and sounded
so distant even to the woman that mouthed them.

Ida sobbed as she lifted her shoulders to capture a breath.
"Oh Becca, Becca . . ."

Amy sat on her father's shoulders with chubby legs around
his neck as she clung tightly to his big hands lifted above his
head to steady his little girl. They walked to the big corral and
Amy giggled as she watched the cowboy try to spur the
mustang into submission. The bony bronc and six more like
him were new additions to the ranch remuda and the task of
breaking the mounts to ride had fallen to a new vaquero, Jorgé.
Other cowboys sat on the top rail of the corral's pole fence and
cheered the vaquero on in his efforts. With feet deep in the
stirrups and a firm grip on the braided lead-rope, the vaquero
rode the tiring mount like a rocking chair. Every dip of the
mustang's head was countered with a deep seat and lean-back
of the rider. When the mustang kicked his hind feet at the
clouds, the vaquero let loose a "Yeeeehaaawww!" and dug in
the spurs. Amy giggled at the spectacle and J.W. let a broad
smile cross his worried face. Soon the mustang tired and quit
bucking and with a couple running laps around the corral he
stood splay legged, head down and sucking wind. Jorge´
stepped down and tossed the lead rope to a handler and walked
to the fence to rest his head on his arms and gather his share of
the dusty wind.

As J.W. turned to resume his walk, he was stopped by a
touch on his elbow. Looking around he saw Sean standing by
his side, "I thought I'd warn you, Pa ain't happy you're here so
if I were you, I'd try to lay low as much as possible."

"Yeah, I figgered as much, me'n pistol here," nodding with
his head that had tiny fingers in his hair, ". . .we'll just hang
around out here. Might even go for a ride to keep her busy,"
answered J.W.

With a nod of acknowledgement, Sean stepped to the fence and took a seat on the top rail to watch the continuing action with the new mustangs. J.W. started his walk around the grounds that brought back fond memories of the many stolen rendezvous with Flo when they were courting. Reaching up with both hands he carefully brought Amy down to the ground and the tall man and the little lady slowly strolled around the old path of memories. Amy reached down to pick up a shiny rock that caught her eye and J.W. smiled at the innocence and curiosity of the child. *She's gonna be a beauty with that curly blonde hair and those dimples and she's gonna be just like her mother, always curious about everything.* J.W. enjoyed every moment he had with his child, he still marveled at the thought that he was a father. It wasn't that long ago that he was alone and aimlessly riding cross country and wondering what he was going to do with his life. Now here he was, a husband and a father, and he couldn't be happier. His thoughts turned to Flo and he felt for her, remembering when he cradled his mother's head in his lap and she told him good-bye. His mother wasn't sick like Rebecca, she was just broken-hearted at the loss of the only love she'd ever known, his father. But now that he knew what that kind of love was, he no longer faulted his mother for leaving him alone. He thought *I don't know if I could stand losing my wife either, and it's gotta be harder for a woman.*

As he turned the corner around the back of the barn he suddenly came face-to-face with McPherson. The big red and grey bearded man held out the flat of his palm in front of him and said, "You stop right there!" and without giving J.W. a chance to respond, continued, "I know you're here with my daughter and I promised my woman I'd do nothin' to ye whilst you're here, but I'm tellin' ye to your face, if anything, anything at all, ever happens to my daughter, I will personally tear you limb from limb and ye can be certain I'll enjoy the doin' of it!" J.W. stood silent as the old man ranted but as the big man turned his back on J.W., Amy started crying and with uplifted arms sought the protection of her daddy.

Florence said later that she thought her mother just held on long enough to see her and Aunt Ida before she passed. Her mother cautioned her to walk softly around her father, she said, "He's still so bitter, it's that thing with fathers and their first born sons. He always expected Patrick to take over the ranch and then everything changed." Flo started to interrupt her mother but the frail figure shushed her with, "I know, I know, it's not J.W.'s fault, Patrick drove him to it and your father was just as much to blame, coming to the church like they did, but that doesn't change the way your father feels, so please, sweetie, just you and J.W. be careful, O.K.?"

"Of course mother, of course. We don't want anything to happen and we'll do our best to stay away." But at the saying of it, Flo knew she was not just losing her mother, she was losing her entire family. The two brothers would be forced to side with their father and nothing would change that but the thought of her family turning their back on her brought a choking sob to Flo as she clung to the bony hand at the side of the bed.

It was a quiet ride home. Flo doted on Amy as she sat with Aunt Ida in the back seat of the buggy. Sean and J.W. were immersed in private thoughts as they shared the front seat with Sean occasionally slapping the rump of the team with the reins more from absentmindedness than any need to encourage the horses. Sean had always been the sensible brother and he knew the confrontation had been the result of Patrick's insane quest for vengeance and his father's misdirected anger.

But even though the shooting was years past, the loss and anger were a constant reminder in his father's mind. His temperament had taken on a bitter edge and the once quiet and thoughtful father had become a temperamental tyrant. Even Hoppy, the even tempered ramrod had quit the ranch. He said as he left, "You've let your loss eat at you like a canker and you've become something I can't abide. I'll not treat men the

187

way you have and if any of 'em have enough backbone, they'll be leavin' you too." The old man just ordered his loyal ramrod from his property and refused to see what he'd become.

Flo seated herself at the table after putting Amy to bed on the trundle. J.W. was nursing the last cup of coffee after the long day of traveling. She reached across the table to grasp her husband's hand and smile at her somber partner. He looked at her and started, "Babe, I'm so sorry you lost your Mum. I know how it hurts and I just wish I could do something to make the hurt go away."

"I know sweetheart, I know, but it was good that we were there when she passed. She made me promise that we'd walk softly concerning Pa, and I said we would. I think that hurts just as much, because I not only lost my Mum, but the rest of my family as well."

J.W. rose from his chair, walked to the side of his wife, kneeled by her side and wrapped his arms around her as she placed her head on his shoulder. The couple stayed still and silent as their hearts beat together with the emotion of the loss. Suddenly, Flo pulled her head back and looking directly at her surprised husband said, "But I have some good news! We're having another baby!" The announcement made J.W. lean back, lose his balance and fall spread-eagled on the floor. Scrambling up to look at his giggling wife he said, "Really?" and at the enthusiastic nodding of his wife he scooped her up and swung her around the room with feet flying but her cheek tight to his. They laughed together and the happiness displaced the sorrow in a home full of love and expectancy of good things to come.

J.W. started the very next day to add another room to their cozy cabin. With a growing family he felt the children would need a separate room and as the couple discussed, one more wouldn't be nearly enough. Their neighbors, Sally and Peter Brooke, were excited for them and were quick to join in the work of adding another room. Aunt Ida had been at the bedside of her dying sister when Flo shared the news of the new baby and now spent much of her free time with the expectant parents. Ida and her husband were unable to have children of their own and Ida doted on her niece and grand-niece, Amy. She busied herself knitting baby afghans and outfits and talked incessantly with Flo about the coming baby.

Another Spring baby arrived while his father was busy in the field. He idly worked more to stay out of the way of the women than to accomplish anything in the field, for some reason he was pre-occupied with the coming of a new child. Nelson Porter Harpold bounced into the world protesting as loudly as his little lungs would allow. J.W. was certain he heard the baby's protestations over and above the braying of his team of mules. When he arrived back at the cabin, he was met at the door with a blanketed bundle that appeared to be all mouth as he still proclaimed his entrance into the world. But a broad smile from a proud father overcame all the protests when he was told he had a son. His smile spread so wide he couldn't even speak when pride and joy filled him as he seated himself at the bedside of his pale but smiling wife. The doctor, Aunt Ida, and Sally stood aside and beamed at the proud parents. Little Amy stepped beside her father and looked at the now snoozing boy and said, "He's noisy!" to the laughter of the entire room.

Chapter Thirty-One

Changes

IDA HAD BECOME more of a sister and very good friend than an Aunt. Both women enjoyed their times together and those times were most often spent tending to the children. As was typical of the times, the work was never done and with two busy children, the couple enjoyed life. Whatever they couldn't provide in 'extras' for the children, Ida never hesitated to supply the necessary goodies to properly spoil her favorite niece and nephew. Occasionally Flo would protest but was easily won over by the persuasive aunt with her argument, "Now Flo, you know we love these kids as if they were our own, so don't deprive me of the blessing of spoiling them like a grandma."

J.W. had cleared another ten acres that were now providing an additional crop of corn for the livestock. His growing herd now numbered twenty-five and he was proud of his home place. They were starting their fifth year and J.W. leaned on the fence post as he surveyed his fields and crops and cattle. He often wished his parents had lived to see what their son had become and to enjoy their grandchildren, but such was not to be and life would go on. Amy trotted her Shetland pony up to her father with a broad smile as she bounced on the wide back of the pony. The little gelding was a dark chestnut with flaxen mane and a gentle personality and loved Amy as much as the girl treasured her pony. J.W. watched the bouncing bundle of joy as she approached and smiled broadly with pride, not even four years old and as her mother would say, "She rides that pony better'n a wild Indian!"

"Hi Daddy!" she squealed in her tiny voice and added, "Momma says lunch is ready and for you to come home right now!" J.W. smiled at the commanding remark from his little girl with the long blonde curls and answered, "O.K. sweetheart, but I don't think there's room on Buster for the both of us, do you?"

"No, but Momma says you have long legs and that you'd probly beat me back to the house. Come'on, I'll race ya!" and without waiting for a response from her father, she reined the chestnut around and with legs flopping high, trotted the Shetland back to the house. J.W. chuckled as he watched the little girl in boy's britches throw her leg over the back of the pony and slide easily to the ground. It was more of a challenge to her to mount the steps to the porch than it was to mount her pony, but she made it and stood with hands on hips as she watched her daddy jog up to the cabin. He bent over with hands on his knees and sucked air, then stood up and said, "You beat me!" Amy giggled and ran into the house. J.W. followed his favorite daughter into the warm cabin and greeted his wife with a big hug and a kiss.

J.W. had carefully crafted a high chair for his daughter when she just one-year-old and now that same chair was occupied by her chubby cheeked tousle headed brother that already had a head start on the rest of the family with his lunch. The mashed potatoes and gravy were spread from ear to ear and even in his eyebrows. He smiled and showed the two new teeth on his lower gum as he beat on the tray with his wooden spoon. Mom, Dad and Sister all laughed at the spectacle of the potato boy and pulled out their chairs for their meal. J.W. had

191

packed a family Bible with him since he left the graveside of his father and it now served as a booster seat for his daughter. Reaching out to grasp the hand of his wife and his daughter, J.W. began his prayer of thanksgiving, not just for the meal, but for the many blessings his family enjoyed.

Leaning back and patting his full stomach, J.W. grinned at his wife and said, "So, what's for desert? Ya gotta a pie or sumpin'?"

"Nope, I've got something better," she declared but didn't elaborate.

"Better? What's better'n a cherry pie fresh from the oven?"

"Oh, something," she added with her familiar mischievous smile as she finished the potatoes and gravy on her plate by giving the last bite to Nelson. Then wiping her hands on her apron, she stood and went to her husband motioning him to pull back from the table and as he complied she sat on his lap with her arms around his neck and smiled at him and said, "I love you," and kissed him.

"Well, I like your kisses an' all, but is that desert?"

"Oh you, always thinkin' about eatin'," she giggled like she used to during their courting days. J.W. smiled and hugged her tight and as her lips were near his ear she whispered, "We're going to have another baby!"

He pushed her back slightly so he could look her in the eye and smiled big and pulled her back for another lingering hug. "When, when's it due?"

"Oh, just like the other two, sometime in the Spring," she said trying in vain to contain her happiness. She had often said she wanted a big family and now with number three on its way, she couldn't restrain her joy.

The months passed slowly as the preparations for the new addition took on their own flavor and tenor. J.W. thought he should get busy with adding another room but Florence said it would be best to wait. "We have plenty of room and Nelson will join his sister in the other bedroom, the baby'll be with us for several months and even after that, he'll sleep in the trundle with us, so, let's just wait before we do all that." With his usual condescending manner, J.W. agreed and focused his energies on repairing the bassinet and building a new frame for the well-used baby bed. After considering the time and the size of Nelson, he thought they would need another high chair and set about plying his skills to the new task. Florence would often visit him in his workshop in the barn and she enjoyed the smells of fresh turned wood and just watching her husband lovingly craft the new chair. She said, "You know, after you're done with that, you could make me a new rocking chair so I can be comfortable while I'm nursing the new baby. There's just something about rocking while I'm holding a baby that makes things, well, feel so right. I would love to have one, could you?"

J.W. had stopped his work and stood to look at his wife standing with one hand at her back and the other resting on her growing belly and replied, "Of course. If I knew you felt that way, I'd have made you one 'fore now. Why didn't you tell me?"

"Well, you were so busy and all with the crops and such, and then the Brooke's fire, and all. It just wasn't important to me then," she smiled as she explained. J.W. looked back at his project and thought a while, calculating work and time, and said, "I believe I'll have just enough time, that is if you don't get in a hurry with the new one," as he motioned to her belly. She smiled back at her husband and said, "Well, it's not up to me, and the way he's been actin' I wouldn't be surprised if he does get in a hurry." She knew every pregnancy was unique and the different pains and sickness she felt with this one were not alarming but a little concerning. She turned to fetch the children from their play in the yard, they were chasing some wild cotton tail bunny rabbits around, and get them ready for bed. She was looking forward to a good night's rest as well.

As the time drew near, Florence found it more difficult to get around. This time was different, it wasn't that she was especially large but she attributed it to the way she was carrying this child. Whenever mothers would get together their conversation often turned to childbearing and the labor and birthing of their children and Florence had been in those same discussions where all the women agreed that every pregnancy was unique. Aunt Ida couldn't give any advice or counsel since she had never borne a child, but she was very attentive to her niece's needs and continually did everything she could to care for her. It had become a daily routine for Ida to drive her new buggy, often referred to as a doctor's buggy, with the high stepping blaze faced bay mare in harness, to visit the Harpold home. On this visit she said, "I'm not going anywhere. I'll make me a pallet right here in front of the fireplace and I'll be here when you need me. You can't get out of bed to tend to the children so that's my job now, and don't argue with me, you know I'm right."

Flo just flashed a feeble smile and nodded her head to agree. She was relieved that Ida would be staying because she was getting a little apprehensive and even nervous about the coming birth. She didn't know why she felt that way, there had been nothing to alarm her, but she was more anxious than ever before.

A gasp and a muffled scream startled Ida awake and she immediately jumped up and ran to the bedroom. Florence was on her side holding her stomach and grimacing in pain. J.W. asked, "Is it time? You want me to get the doctor?" Florence nodded her head and he quickly ran from the room dragging his britches, shirt and boots. He hurriedly dressed as he ran stumbling for the barn to get his horse. After he left, Flo flipped the covers back to reveal a puddle of water and blood behind her. She looked at Ida with fear in her eyes and a question on her face. Ida ran to get the stack of rags that awaited this event and returning dabbed at the mess, put some fresh flower sacking behind and under Flo and eased her back on the stack of pillows. Flo said, "Light the fire so Sally will see, I know J.W. will forget." Ida nodded her head and ran to the door. As she opened the door the already lit fire showed the retreating form of J.W. as he spurred his horse to a full run for the doctor. Another scream from Flo brought Ida back to her side as she saw the mother-to-be clutching a pillow to her contorted face as she tried to muffle the scream that fought its way free. She didn't want to alarm her children but it was too late as a sleepy eyed Amy stood in the doorway asking, "Is mommy all right?"

"Your mommies gonna be fine, we think the new baby might be on its way, so you go back and cuddle with your brother, O.K.?" She nodded her head and dragging her rag doll, returned to her bed with Nelson still fast asleep. Ida had put the two to bed together because Nelson had fallen asleep while they were playing, but she realized now how beneficial that would prove to be. Ida buzzed around like a jealous hornet protecting her nest, but it was all she could do to keep Florence reassured. Twice more she had to change the bedding and the pile of bloody rags and bedding grew. Finally, the doctor arrived and instructed J.W. to stay outside. Sally had already opted to take the children back to her house as she could tell things weren't going right and it would be no place for the children. So she and her husband, Peter, bundled them up and with Sally in the back with them, Peter drove the buckboard the short distance to their home. Elijah gladly surrendered his bed to the younger children and after they were settled in, he joined his parents at the table. Without any hesitation, the family joined hands and bowed their heads in prayer for their friends and neighbors.

The pale grey clouds obscured the rising sun as the start of the day was made somber with the lack of blue sky and sunshine. Sally stood on the porch and looked in the distance at her friend's house and there was no sign of any activity at all. She turned back to her kitchen and spoke to her husband, "Peter, I think it would be a good thing for you to go over and be a friend to J.W., I'm thinkin' things aren't going right. But if everything's O.K. you can come back and get us, O.K.?"

"Sure thing, pumpkin, whatever you think's right. I'll get my horse and head on over there." Nothing more was said as she waved to her husband as he left their front yard enroute to the neighbors.

But before Peter arrived, the doctor summoned J.W. inside. Placing his hand on the taller man's shoulder the doctor said, "I'm sorry, I've done all I can, but she's lost too much blood. The baby's fine, but you don't have much time."

J.W. felt like he'd been stomped on by the meanest bronc in the country, his knees started to buckle and he grabbed at the doctor's shoulder for support. With tears welling in his eyes he asked, "You mean...?"

"Yes, she won't make it. Now try to be strong for her and sit with her. Go 'head on now. Go to her, she needs you."

Taking a deep breath and trying to stand tall, he stumbled a little but righted himself and walked into the bedroom with a forced smile on his face. Seeing the pale face of his wife, he almost collapsed against the wall but steadied himself and knelt by her bedside. He gently took her hand in his and looked at his beloved. She smiled and said, "We have another son, and as we agreed, I've named him William Cody." He smiled as he remembered their discussion about names as they sat at the table and held hands. Then with her smile slipping away she said, "Remember what we talked about? If anything happened to either of us and about the children? Do you remember?" J.W. nodded his head and squeezed her hand as he choked back the tears that were blinding him. He used his sleeve to wipe them away and with a sob said, "I remember."

"Good, and I want you to always remember I love you, and I don't regret a day we've had together. And sweetheart, about my father . . . " her words were interrupted by a stabbing pain as she grabbed at her waist and looked at J.W. with fear. She slowly relaxed and turned her head back to her husband and with a smile said, "I love you."

Chapter Thirty-Two

Separation

THE YARD WAS FULL of buggies and wagons and several saddle horses were tethered to the rail of the corral. It was a good sized crowd of neighbors, friends and church family that gathered by the grave site at the edge of the woods behind the house. The slight hill offered a view of the valley below and the pastor stood at the head of the grave as he started to close his message. "Beloved, we can rest assured that our dear sister and friend is in Heaven today. I'm sure she was welcomed into the arms of Jesus as she entered that wonderful eternal home. But I want you to know, she isn't in Heaven because she earned her way by being a good wife and mother, although she was that. And she's not in Heaven because she was a church goer, although she was a faithful member of the church. No, we are certain she's in Heaven today because there was a time in her life that she realized her need of a Savior and she bowed her head and asked Jesus to give her that gift of eternal life that He paid for on the cross. And true to His promise that "*Whosoever shall call upon the name of the Lord, shall be saved.*" (Rom. 10:13) Jesus gave her that gift of eternal life and ushered her

197

into Heaven." He concluded the service with prayer and every one made their way to shake hands with J.W. and express their condolences.

Many well-wishers had brought dishes of food and the table was loaded with a variety of goods. Several stayed for a while, but soon the house was empty except for Ida, Sally, Peter and the children. Elijah was playing the big brother and ushered the children outside to spend some time together in the shade of the big oak tree. Sally gave J.W. a lingering hug, looked at him and gave another quick hug and turned away. Peter shook J.W.'s hand and said, "If there's anything, anything at all..." J.W. shook his head in understanding and followed his friends to the door. He stood on the step and watched as they pulled away in their buckboard. Amy and the toddler, Nelson, stood on either side of their dad and held onto his trousers.

They struggled through an evening meal put together by Ida and as she cleaned up a mite, J.W. put the kids in bed. They would sleep together again tonight. As Ida finished her puttering with the various dishes and wiping the counter and table, she finally sat down beside her somber nephew. He looked up at her and reached out his hand for hers. Slowly he began, "I know Flo talked to you about it before, but I need to make sure you understand. When we, Flo and I, agreed, I never thought it would ever happen, but here we are. If it wasn't for her father, old man McPherson, things would be different, better, but he is such a bitter old man. You see, I promised Flo I would never raise a hand to her father, she just couldn't stand the thought that I might be forced to fight him like I was forced to fight Patrick. And her greatest fear was that something could happen to the children, and we both agreed we could never allow that. If I stayed, you know that old man would come stormin' in here and do his best to put my lights out. In his words he said, 'I'll tear you limb from limb!'" and as he stammered, Ida squeezed his hand and interrupted with, "I know, I know. He's a mean old man and he's beyond any reason."

J.W. said, "Let me finish. When we talked about it, you know, if anything should happen we agreed we wanted you and your husband to take the kids," she started to interrupt again but he continued, "I think it would be best if you moved out here and took over the ranch. It's a good place and the only home the kids have known. Your husband can drive into town easy enough and you'll have the place to yourself, with the kids of course. If I'm around, that old man'll just do his darndest to keep his promise and the kids don't need to be subjected to that. 'Sides, you and I both know I wouldn't be able to take care of 'em and especially with the new one and all. Without Flo, I'm useless around the kids. I love 'em with all my heart and it breaks my heart to think of leavin' but I really don't see as I have any choice in the matter. Now, we both agreed on this and I know you'll be a great mother to 'em and they deserve the best and you're it!" He dropped his head on his arms and wept. After a while when he gathered himself a mite, he said to Ida, "I'll be back in a little bit." As he left the room, he touched the back of the new rocking chair and set it to rocking, empty.

He walked back to the grave with the moonlight showing the way. He stood at the foot of the grave for a moment, then fell prone on the newly turned soil and wept again. "What am I going to do without you, I can't make it without you." Then propping himself on his elbows he dabbed at his tears with his shirtsleeve and looked up at the quarter moon that hung from a silver lined cloud and cried, "Why God? Why did you have to take her?" As the sliver of moon disappeared behind a larger cloud, the blackness of the night wrapped the grieving man in its cloak of darkness and held him close.

J.W. tethered the steel dust and the bay pack horse to the rail in front of the house and stepped up on the porch. Retrieving his Sharps and saddle bags, he slipped the rifle into the scabbard and tied on the saddle bags. His bedroll was behind the saddle and the packs were tight on the pack frame.

He stood with one hand on the rump of his horse and let his eyes rove the fields and the memories. *Sure is different than when we rode up that overgrown road that first day. Don't look nuthin' like it did, it's a nice place now and it'll be a good place for the kids.* He dropped his head, stepped to the rose bushes and with his knife cut an armful of new blossoms and buds. He walked back to the grave, arranged the flowers at the head and knelt on one knee to say a last good bye. *Well, Babe, I guess this is good bye. It wasn't supposed to be like this, but . . . well, I'm sure the kids'll be fine, you know Ida really loves 'em and she'll probably spoil 'em rotten, but it's for the best. You know I'll always love you and we'll be together some day, maybe soon. I love you.* He stood, blew her a kiss and walked back to the house.

Ida stood on the porch with a child on each side grasping her skirt. They watched their dad as he walked from behind the house and up to the steps of the porch. He stretched out a long leg and knelt beside Amy, taking her in his arms for a big hug. He couldn't stop the tears as they streamed down his face but he held on to his daughter not wanting to ever let her go. Finally, as the little girl said, "Daddy, you're crying. Don't cry."

He leaned back so he could look at his precious child and said, "I'm sorry sweetheart, I'm just sad because I have to go away and I can't stand the thought of not being able to hold you tight every night!" as he forced a smile from behind the tears. He watched as tiny tears welled up in her eyes. He forced himself to turn away and look to his son. The toddler held tight to Ida's skirt and buried his face in the folds of material. With his dad tugging at his arm he turned to see his dad and held out his tiny arms for a hug. J.W. grabbed him up and stood up to hold his son to his chest with a big hug. With another squeeze, he stood the boy beside his aunt and stepped to his horse. Without saying anymore, he swung up on his big grey that side-stepped with an anxious nod. He said to his children, "Always remember, Daddy loves you." He pulled the reins and pivoted his horse on his hind legs and lightly touched his spurs to the grey's ribs to start his journey to a destination unknown.

The little children waved at their disappearing daddy and he could barely hear, "Don't leave Daddy, please," from his favorite daughter, the little girl with dimples and long blonde curls whose image was forever imprinted on his mind right beside the mischievous grin of the toddler. And once again, he was ridin' lonesome.

Notes From The Author

Ridin' Lonesome is based on the true story of my grandfather. Yes, he really did have a shoot-out at the church picnic with his future brother in law and yes James Enoch McPherson threatened to kill him. I did however, take literary license in setting the story fifty years farther in the past than it actually happened. Also, the Harpolds were actually neighbors to the McPhersons and J.W. and Florence grew up together, but that's not as exciting as meeting a new cowboy, so it changed a little. The only other change was when J.W. left. J.W. and Florence were actually together about twenty years and when she died, J.W. left but Amy was already married to my father, Carl Rundell. The boys, Nelson, William (Cody), and Raymond moved in with Amy until they were older and left to start their own homes. When J.W. left, the only word the family received was that he had died three years later in Arkansas. However, that proved erroneous when our family was contacted by a John McCabe Junior. Come to find out, J.W. changed his name to McCabe, went to Kansas, started a farm, remarried and had another family. I didn't find this out until after his death when his son, John Jr., attempting to put together his family tree discovered the subterfuge. It was verified by my Uncle (William)Cody Harpold when the scar from the shoot-out on my grandfather's forearm was identified. So, don't search out your genealogy if you're not prepared for surprises. Thanks to all my readers, I hope you enjoyed the story!

A look at To Keep a Promise by B.N. Rundell

The power of a promise made and a promise kept is realized when Jeremiah Thompsett comes of age and accepts the responsibility of fulfilling his mentor's long-held dream. Raised by an escaped slave in the midst of the Arapaho nation in the Wind River mountains, he now must track down the slave catchers that killed his adopted father and stole their cache. The Vengeance Quest takes him and his companions through the mountains and across the nation to fulfill the promise of freeing the family of slaves held dear to his mentor and adopted father.

Accompanied by Broken Shield and Laughing Waters, his Arapaho friend and his sister, the trek through the mountains and to Fort Union is fraught with hazard and ambush. It is here he is joined by Scratch, the crusty mountain man who joins him on his journey downriver and across country to find Ezekiel's family and to seek to free them.

About the Author

Born and raised in Colorado into a family of ranchers and cowboys, B.N. is the youngest of seven sons. Juggling bull riding, skiing, and high school, graduation was a launching pad for a hitch in the Army Paratroopers. After the army, he finished his college education in Springfield, MO, and together with his wife and growing family, entered the ministry as a Baptist preacher.

Together, B.N. and Dawn raised four girls that are now married and have made them proud grandparents. With many years as a successful pastor and educator, he retired from the ministry and followed in the footsteps of his entrepreneurial father and started a successful insurance agency, which is now in the hands of his trusted nephew. He has also been a successful audiobook narrator and has recorded many books for several award-winning authors. Now finally realizing his life-long dream, B.N. has turned his efforts to writing a variety of books, from children's picture books and young adult adventure books, to the historical fiction and western genres which are his first love

Discover more great titles by B. N. Rundell and Wolfpack Publishing at:
http://wolfpackpublishing.com/b-n-rundell/